GODS OF SMOKE AND STARS

Seeds of Chaos
Book 4

AZALEA ELLIS

To Jared.
Though the shadows grow long.

Chapter 1

I watched with interest as the craggy stone of the chasm walls sped past. The sun beat down through the distant cleft of the ravine. Its blinding brightness threw distinct shadows off the jagged rocks and heated us even through the protection of the ship's hull.

Small creatures turned to watch us from the shaded nooks and crannies they'd hidden themselves in, even their quick reflexes too slow to do more than take notice as we shot by. The distant floor of the ravine, channeling only the barest trickle of water, rose upward as the chasm widened.

Through a trick of perspective, it looked like the rough walls rushed away from my perch at the port-side viewing window into the distance, though in truth the canyon was simply widening and growing more shallow as we approached the mouth. Even as I had this thought, our little ship reached the end, flying out over a massive, dry seabed. I could not see far before everything became obscured by the haze of smoke in the air.

"We're here," I said, leaning closer to the window as we zoomed over a sprawling mass of tents and stalls. The only area clear of people was the far side of the dry seabed, which I could barely make out.

It seemed to be covered in growths and broken by a glass-shatter pattern of smaller chasms. The seabed ended abruptly where huge buttes broke free of the plain. A splash of greenery crowned each butte, the only vegetation in sight.

Zed bounced over, shoving his face up against the window with a grin. "Finally! Is that the Trial arena? Wow, so many people. Are they all here for the tournament, too? Where's the god?"

Kris came over to watch too, directing her new marionette, which was still a work in progress, to hold her tiny form up to the window so she could see out.

Adam frowned and rubbed his bloodshot eyes. "I just want to get off this damn ship. Why did we even agree to this visit in the first place?"

Gregor nodded emphatically, his arms crossed over his small chest. "I vote we don't accept any more visits to places that don't have Shortcuts. This was the most boring road trip I've ever been on." Despite his words, he sidled subtly over to the window nearest himself and peeked out with poorly disguised interest.

I pressed the pads of my clawed fingers into the muscle at the base of my neck, trying to relieve some stiffness. I knew Adam and Gregor were just grumpy because it seemed the diplomatic missions we'd been on were never-ending. Estreyer had more levels and scattered pockets of civilization than I'd realized. Every sect of the Estreyan world wanted a visit from the godkiller and the members of the Seal of Nine, and Queen Mardinest pushed us to accept their requests as a show of good-will. She hoped our fame would help offset some of the tension and animosity our collaboration with Earth had stirred up among her rivals, and more allies were always good.

Jacky rolled her eyes at the others, despite the fact that she too had grumbled her way through the entire trip, constantly asking how long it would be till we arrived and challenging everyone to arm wrestling matches. She'd grown so bored she'd taken to using Zed as a workout weight.

My brother had sat on her back while she did single-finger pushups, then he pretended to be superman flying around while she lifted him with her feet and walked on her hands.

Adam had become so annoyed by their antics that he'd made a straight-jacket out of ink to confine Jacky.

I'd thought things might escalate at that point and had been ready to step in, but instead of growing angry, Jacky was delighted. This struggle turned into a new game; Jacky's strength pitted against Adam's restraints, for a surprisingly even match.

Sam sighed in relief and turned to me. "Uh, do you think we might be able to get a bigger ship next time? One with multiple rooms so we're not cooped up together?"

"Definitely. I should have realized this ship would be a problem as soon as they brought it around."

Adam grumbled something about how cheap royalty could be, but Torliam ignored him, sulking silently as he shot glares toward the cockpit.

Queen Mardinest had insisted, despite Torliam's protests, that one of our guards pilot the craft instead of her son. Now the man flew us across the pop-up city, doing a valiant job of ignoring Torliam's jealousy.

The ship slowed once it reached the fancier tents, which lay at the north of the city on either side of the green-topped buttes. Our pilot opened the door on the side, and, after a couple moments to gather our things, my team and I jumped out onto the hard-packed dirt.

The scorching air swept stinging ash into my eyes, and I had to squint to look around. We were near one of the main streets, and plenty of people bustled about despite the heat of the day and the warmth of the very earth radiating into the air. It was like standing in a pot on the stove.

The people, dressed in loose, light-colored clothing that

wrapped around their bodies to protect them from the sun, pointed and stared at us, quickly forming into a crowd and disturbing traffic.

Kris hunched her shoulders instinctively, clearly nervous to parade herself before these strangers, but then straightened and turned to the gathering throng. She gave them a small wave, a strained smile on her face.

They broke out into cheers, waving back at the tiny girl, and some of her embarrassment melted away.

Gregor pressed the back of his hand dramatically to his forehead. "This temperature is inhumane." He squinted around, sighed, and slipped into his Shadow state.

The crowd loved that even more.

I wished *I* had a Skill that let me negate the heat and simultaneously avoid interacting with people. My scales lifted a little to let air flow closer to my skin. I didn't bother to smile or wave to the crowd, merely dipped my chin to them in a perfunctory nod. Luckily, my public persona, especially on Estreyer, relied more on awe and having cured the Sickness than exuding any sense of amiability or approachability.

"Isn't someone supposed to meet us here?"

As if summoned by my words, a wiry man with wrinkled, tanned skin bustled up to the ship, sidling his way through the crowd. His clothes were more brightly colored than most, embroidered around the edges with complicated designs. He chattered non-stop while gesturing widely with his arms.

"Welcome! The people of Shaddah greet you, Godkiller. Thank you for blessing our humble land with your presence. I am sure it will bring good luck to those who fight for water. I am Fanir, one of the organizers of the night market and the Trial tournament. Come, we have prepared accommodations for you. You have arrived just in time. The first round of the blood games will begin tomorrow." He waved for us to follow and scurried off down the packed-dirt road.

We followed through streets lined with vendors selling

souvenirs and snacks. Occasionally, they even sold water, which commanded ridiculous prices. Sam frowned, tugging at the straps of his pack. "If water's that scarce, how are you able to grow crops here? Do people hunt for all their food?"

Fanir laughed. "They are hocking their water at such high prices now because they know that in three days, when the Trial is completed and the water of the Well is released to our people, no one will be willing to buy it. It has been three years since the last Bestowal."

Birch's nose twitched as he scampered around, sniffing the air. His second eyelid was closed against the ash, giving his green, human-shaped irises a milky film. His ears perked up and he turned toward one stall, where a man was roasting plump lizards on sticks. Birch ran over to him and stood on his hind legs, holding himself up with his front paws against the edge of the stall. He let out a whine, eyes trained on the lizard currently being cooked.

The vendor's eyes widened and tracked from Birch over to me. The man grinned widely, bowed to me, and handed Birch the skewered lizard.

As Birch grabbed the snack and swaggered back to the group with a positively smug look on his face, Torliam sighed deeply, dug in the money pouch at his waist, and went to pay the vendor for the treat.

Jacky stole one of the lizard's legs from Birch, shoving it in her mouth and running ahead to walk beside Fanir before the winged cat could retaliate. "Is there gonna be betting and stuff on the fights?" she garbled past the hunk of meat.

Adam pinched the bridge of his nose and closed his eyes.

Fanir grinned and gave Jacky a shallow bow while walking. "Yes, Jacky of the Nine, I am pleased to say that we have plenty of wagering opportunities. The betting courts are directly outside the eastern border of the Trial arena. If you wish, I can have a guide come to bring your distinguished self to visit them."

"My distinguished self?" Jacky grinned and slapped Fanir on the shoulder, almost slamming him forward onto the ground. "I like you!"

He gasped for air and clutched at his shoulder but smiled even brighter, seemingly unperturbed. "Perhaps you are also interested in greeting some dignitaries visiting from other lands? Or perhaps you wish to display your strength as warriors. It is not too late to enter the tournament!"

Torliam frowned at the man. "We have not agreed to any other promotional activities. We were told only our presence was requested."

Fanir flushed a little, though it could have been because of the heat. "Of course, of course. I was only making a suggestion for your own enjoyment. You have no obligations."

We arrived at a large, multi-storied tent. Even though the entire structure was made of fabric, the walls and floors were somehow stiff enough to support multiple levels, coming together to create a hotel of sorts. Despite my assumption that I would be able to hear everything going on within the tent, sound was thoroughly muffled as we passed from room to room. Estreyan technology never ceased to amaze me.

Fanir showed us each to a room, assigning the best rooms—the ones with balconies—to Torliam and I, on either end of the topmost level. Then, he left us to our own devices, promising to send a servant with food and come back for us when night fell.

I dug my toes into the carpet and looked out onto the open balcony and the somewhat haphazard sprawl of the streets and tents below. I shrugged off my backpack and dug in it for the Oracle's third gift, still unsolved. Now that I had more time and wasn't dealing with a crisis, I found it relaxing rather than frustrating to work on, though I was beginning to wonder if I would ever solve it. I settled on the shaded divan next to the balcony, letting the breeze cool me.

The door flap opened behind me, and I turned to see a red-headed woman with tan skin and freckles walk in, carrying a tray with a glass of cold water. "Hello, Eve-Redding," she said with a slight smile.

I stood and grinned back, more for the cold water than out of any sense of politeness. "Hello. Thank you."

She bowed politely as I took the water, but didn't leave immediately. "I am here as your guide and attendant. Do you have any plans for entertainment or desires I can help facilitate? The blood games do not happen frequently, so you will wish to take full advantage of this opportunity to experience our culture and amenities."

I drank before answering, then held the glass out for her to take. "I don't have any plans. Do you have any suggestions?"

She held up her platter, allowing me to drop the empty glass on it. "You don't plan to enter the tournament? The Trial is an important part of our culture, and you are a powerful warrior. Surely, you do not fear the danger?"

I resisted the urge to roll my eyes. Why did all the Estreyans I'd met so far on this level want me to take part in the Trial? Wouldn't the god's Bestowal of water be sufficient without help?

"I've had plenty of fighting. Enough to last me a lifetime. There's no reason to put myself in danger when there are plenty of other warriors happy to do so in my stead." Something inside me stirred at the words, but I ignored it, pushing the feeling back down.

It was true. I *didn't* want to fight, I repeated mentally.

She nodded. "I thought as much." Something in her tone was off.

Before I could pursue that thought, the room swirled around me. I tried to focus on her face, but instead, I found myself tripping and falling back onto the divan. Colors swam through the air and the light twisted, making it seem like the world was a photo negative of itself, wherever the shadows existed. My head pounded.

Something neon purple and made of shifting tentacles rose

out of the shadows underneath the divan. Its limbs wrapped around my own and held me down. "The sparkly thing she was playing with earlier," a new voice said, high-pitched and distorted. "Grab it."

She leaned over me, reaching past my collapsed form. Unnatural green light seemed to glow from her eyes in the not-light of the shadows.

I reached for Chaos, and it bubbled up around me, dizzy and sluggish.

She drew back before I had the chance to attack, something sparkly surrounding her fist with halo-like lines. My puzzle band, still unsolved. She was taking it. Stealing it.

"Nno," I slurred, even as the purple tentacles withdrew, retreating into the shadows below me. I tried to get up, to lash at her with Chaos, to do anything to stop her.

She paused, staring down at me with a complete lack of concern. From the edges of the room, under the furniture, and behind the curtains, little glowing beige and green fairies appeared. Sand formed their bodies, and lizard skin their clothes. They chittered brightly as they surrounded her.

She stepped backward into the deeper shadow against the wall, and with a flash like a black light in the darkness, they were all gone. Though she had vanished, the light around me remained distorted.

My dizziness grew. Blackness dropped over my eyes like a shroud, and I slipped into unconsciousness.

Chapter 2

I woke up with a pounding head and a tongue that felt too big for my mouth and tasted like rancid meat. I dry heaved a couple times, wondering if I'd suddenly developed a taste for hard alcohol the night before, because I was pretty sure I was experiencing an extreme hangover.

Then I remembered what had happened and fell off the divan, landing on the cloth floor on my hands and knees.

I checked frantically for the puzzle band but didn't find it, either with my eyes or with Wraith.

It was really gone.

—I need your help. Hurry.—
-Eve-

I SENT the message in a Window to my teammates, even as Wraith exploded out from me, unfurling through the air to search the streets for almost a mile in every direction. I found thousands of spots of power and rifled through them like a mental deck of cards, looking for one I recognized. Some of them were Estreyans with a high amount of Seeds, and quite a few were objects that glowed with a light of their own, but none of them were the Oracle's third gift, the largest puzzle band.

Adam, who had been closest, burst into the room first, throwing aside the flap of noise-cancelling fabric that made up the door. "What's wrong?"

"Someone stole the Oracle's third gift," I said simply, sparing a bit of concentration from my search for the thief and my property. "It's been…" I paused to check the angle of the shadows falling on the street outside. "Hours already."

My other teammates piled into the room behind Adam, calming when they saw I wasn't hurt.

"How did this happen?" Torliam said, scanning me from head to toe.

"It was the guide Fanir sent to show us around. Or at least that's who she said she was. She drugged me, I think. I drank a glass of water she gave me."

"*Fanir*," Adam said, whirling on one foot. "I'll get him."

I nodded. "Get the enforcers, or whatever passes for them around here. Maybe there's something they can do to track her. I doubt she stuck around. In the meantime, nobody touch anything, in case they can do forensics."

Adam left, taking Jacky with him for backup.

Sam placed his hand on my arm. "Looks like whatever she used is mostly metabolized already, but there are faint traces left. Strong hallucinogenic?"

I nodded and gave Sam a smile of thanks when he took the worst of the side-effects away from me. I turned to Torliam. "Can you find her with your Skill? She had red hair and green eyes, and she had freckles even though her skin was tan."

Torliam grimaced. His eyes went blank as his power flared. He shook his head. "That is not enough familiarity for me to find the thief. Perhaps if I had seen her myself, or knew more about her, I would be able to. However," he paused, and his gaze grew distant again. "I am quite familiar with the Oracle's third gift. It will take some time, but I will find it."

I sighed with relief, some of the tension going out of my shoulders.

"Red hair and green eyes don't sound like the servant that I saw," Zed said. The rest of my teammates confirmed that statement. Though they hadn't all been served by the same person, none of the servants had red hair or green eyes.

We left the room to wait for Adam and Jacky, who returned with Fanir and a small group of Estreyans. From the matching bright red bands around their biceps and their take-charge attitudes, I assumed they were the local law enforcement.

"Someone stole a precious artifact from you?" The speaker, who I took to be the ranking enforcer in this group, wore a frown on his face as his eyes roved over the room. "Please tell me everything that happened, in detail."

I took a deep breath and forced my muscles to relax and my heart rate to slow. My scales settled, and I realized they'd been raised, their sharp edges angled aggressively. I really needed to get a grip on that, or I'd be signaling my emotional state to anyone who knew what to look for. I thought back carefully, and related everything that had happened between getting off the ship and that moment. I'd been unconscious for most of that time, so there wasn't much to tell.

Still, when I got to the part where the thief questioned my intent to join the Trial, the local enforcer turned a suspicious eye on Fanir, who'd asked the same question.

The rest of us followed his gaze.

Fanir paled under the surface of his tan skin and waved his hands frantically at all of us. "It is an understandable question! You are the godkiller, and the mightiest of our warriors find honor in fighting for the prosperity of the land! I do not have any affiliation with this thief. I would never bring such dishonor upon my family. I have nothing to gain from this!"

The enforcer squinted at him. "Please bring all of your staff for questioning." He turned back to me. "Please, continue."

When I finished, the enforcer nodded, then used his datapad

to place a mandatory stop-and-search order on all outgoing ships. "If they have not escaped already, this will make it more difficult to smuggle your artifact out. I will need a sample of your saliva and the skin of your palms. Did anything else come into contact with this glass of water?"

"No." Inside, I berated myself. How could I have been so stupid as to trust her? Why didn't I realize something was off? If she'd wanted to, she could have killed me. "But I doubt there are any traces of the drug remaining. Sam already healed me."

The enforcer sighed, looking into the distance with a put-upon expression.

Sam fidgeted slightly, always a little more awkward without Black Sun active to calm him. "Uh, I might be able to reproduce a version of the hallucinogenic. It won't be exactly the same, but it might help?"

As Sam gave the enforcers a sample, rubbing it on a fuzzy stick with his finger, Zed moved over to me and bumped me with his shoulder, a subtle attempt at comfort. "Is there anyone with a Skill that can help here?" he asked the enforcers. "Do you have security cameras or microphones placed in the streets?"

One of the other enforcers stared at him. "Such devices would be a gross violation of the citizens' privacy. We have no such thing here in Shaddah."

My brother grimaced. "Okay, well, what about someone with a Skill?"

Gregor crossed his arms, obviously unimpressed.

Kris poked Gregor in the side and warned him to "be polite" out of the corner of her mouth.

The enforcer nodded. "We have scent trackers. However…"

Adam groaned aloud, talking over the end of the man's sentence. "All of us packing into the room muddied up the scent trail by now, especially if the thief barely touched anything. Right?"

The man nodded, obviously uncomfortable.

Sam waved his hands at us in a calming motion. "It's okay.

Torliam is tracking the puzzle band right now. We're going to find it, and more than likely we'll find the thief along with it. There's no need to get upset."

Gregor let out a loud sigh and turned to Zed. "Can't you open a rip to the Other Place? I need something to cool me down, and these imbeciles don't even have air conditioning."

The enforcers and Fanir all blanched. "The Other Place? Is that necessary?" Fanir started, but a sharp wave of Torliam's hand silenced him.

"There is a tug," Torliam said. "The Oracle's gift is to the north of us. Not far."

"Bring the ship," I ordered. It would be faster than trying to run through the streets, which were quickly growing more crowded as the sun set and the temperature lowered.

When no one moved, I turned to Fanir and raised an eyebrow.

He let out a small, "oh!" and ran off to get our vehicle. Within minutes, Fanir returned, flying the ship into position next to the nearest balcony. The side hatch slid open, allowing us to jump aboard.

Torliam took over the flight controls from Fanir and sent us hurtling through the air after my stolen puzzle band. We stayed low over the tops of the tents, blowing up dust from the streets in our wake.

Torliam took us right over the Trial arena. Below us, it smoldered constantly, as if the cracks reaching down and the coral-like masses twisting up were all made of hot coal—like the smoking ashes of last night's fire. The smoke and embers shed into the air by the alien arena were enough to obscure visibility.

I thought the thief was hiding somewhere within the arena, but Torliam kept going till he reached the edge of it, then angled sharply upward along the steep wall of one of the buttes.

He slowed at the top, then sent the ship creeping forward into the jungle-like greenery. It was as if we'd entered a different world than the fiery, parched land below.

I could see the evidence of the god all around us. The lush plants grew from ashes, sometimes still smoldering, and the water that wove everywhere in tiny streams didn't seem to prevent random plants from suddenly bursting into flame and burning away. Even if things had looked perfectly normal, the glow of power in the air would have clued me in. "We should probably get out and walk," I said, my voice low. "We don't want to offend the goddess."

Torliam grunted his agreement and gently landed the ship atop an area that was more grey and orange ash than green growth. The goddess might not appreciate us crushing her plants. "We are close," he said.

I spread out my awareness, my eyes watering a little in sympathy despite the fact that they couldn't actually *see* the glow of power all around us. I almost didn't notice my puzzle band past the light radiating out from the center of the butte's self-contained ecosystem.

"I found it," I said. "Doesn't look like the thief is anywhere around, but that doesn't mean she's not here. I may have just hallucinated it, but it's also possible she has a Skill that allows her to mess with physics."

We crept forward until we reached a circular, low-rising wall made of flaky white ash that barely covered the glowing embers underneath the surface. Inside the wall was a pool of water that stretched deep into the butte and was the source of all the little streams.

"The goddess's Well," Fanir whispered, bowing reverently to it.

My puzzle band floated serenely in the center of the Well, along with dozens of other objects.

I wanted to clamber over the edge and grab it out of the water, but the oppressive glow of the goddess' power stopped me. "Is it safe to touch the water?"

The enforcer behind me gasped as if he'd just seen someone kick a puppy.

I frowned, turning to back to the group.

My teammates were on edge but ready for action, while the Estreyans native to this level seemed frozen with awe.

The lead enforcer shook his head adamantly. "The objects here are all offerings to the goddess, Aibhan. It seems the thief has given your artifact to her. It is a part of the Trial, now, and will be used and consumed in exchange for water when the Trial is complete. You cannot take it back."

MY FINGERS FLEXED WITH ANGER. "How the hell can someone else decide to offer up something that belongs to me?"

The enforcer looked away, wiping sweat from his forehead while avoiding my gaze.

I clenched my jaw. "There has to be a way to get it back. It should never have been given in the first place. What happens if I just…take it?"

Jacky's eyes flicked around as she searched for movement in our surroundings. "Let them try and stop you," she said. "Do it."

Fanir shook his head frantically, babbling in a low voice, as if to avoid notice by the goddess. "To steal from the Trial offerings of the goddess would be a grave offense! If the goddess is displeased with us, it may jeopardize the Bestowal of water. Without a hearty Bestowal, the lives of the people on this level are not sustainable. A drought will bring poverty. Those who are wealthy and able to do so will leave. Those who are not able to leave would be lucky to survive the sickness, starvation, and violence that would follow!"

I forced my scales, which had risen again, to lie flat, and kept my voice calm. "Well, I don't want to steal the puzzle band. I would simply like it returned to its rightful owner. Perhaps Aibhan wouldn't mind speaking to me. I am a godling, the progeny of Behelaino, Goddess of Khaos. My name is Eve

Redding." My words rode heavy on the air. "If you would, Aibhan."

The mound around the opening of the pool shifted, lifting away from the ground. Ash and embers shook loose and floated away to reveal the torso of a woman, which flowed into the body of a snake. She slithered around the Well toward us, her coiling, meter-wide body unwinding from the edge of the water and following along behind her.

The native Estreyans fell to their hands and knees, but my team and I simply bowed to greet her. She was a minor goddess, and, though still incredibly powerful, it seemed we had met enough of the greater gods to become jaded.

She stopped in front of me, her torso lifted high enough that she was half-again as tall as me, forcing me to look up sharply to meet her dark eyes. Her voice grated like a heavy smoker's, but it was not unpleasant. I imagined stones rolling along the bottom of a rushing stream, or sand sifting through an hour-glass. "Once given, offerings cannot be returned. However... I have heard you speaking with the mortals. It is a grave offense to steal the treasure of a god, or even a godling. If it were me in your position, I would let fire burn up from the ground till my wrath was known to all, and those who had offended me were naught but ash on the wind."

I smiled, baring my teeth. "Trust me, I am going to hunt them down."

She tilted her head to the side, staring down at me with eyes made of coal. Her mouth stretched into a smile. "Yes. Good. Perhaps you will ascend to godhood as I did, with such burning desire in your heart." She took a deep breath and exhaled, a gust of hot hair billowing out from her. I had to blink away the sting of dry heat and ash. "I was once a godling like you. I struggled mightily, with all my hopes, dreams, and the essence of my soul turned toward success. I became the hope of my people. Now, it has been so long that I barely recall my mortal memories. I see them as if through a haze. Still, I have some nostalgia for that time. If you wish, I will allow you to take your offering back."

Some of the tension went out of my shoulders, and my grin grew a little more genuine. Then she kept talking.

"Due to the breach of covenant, the Trial and subsequent Bestowal will be nullified. I will rest for a time, and return to hold the blood games again in three more cycles."

"No!" "You mustn't!" "Have mercy," came the cries from behind me.

I turned back to the others.

Fanir bowed his head to Aibhan, then looked to me. "If necessary, we will compensate you with an equivalent artifact of power, Eve-Redding. I beg you, please do not do this. The Bestowal is our livelihood."

Torliam shook his head at me.

I sighed. "Is there no other way?"

Aibhan chuckled. "Of course there is. You may win back your treasure in the blood games. The champion is allowed to pick a gift from among all the offerings. Of course, if you wish to compete, you will need to give your own offering, since this one was given by another. All who compete must wager something of worth, though not all who have given an offering must compete."

I ground my teeth together.

"You have until the sun rises tomorrow, godling."

I gave her another shallow bow, though I did not take my eyes from hers. "I hope you enjoy the show," I said, then turned back to the others. "Torliam, contact the capital. I need a treasure taken from the vault where we keep all the gifts people have donated. Get it flown here at top speed. The courier will need to take a racing ship and leave right away if they want to arrive on time."

He smiled. "I have already sent the order, while you were busy clenching your jaw so hard I heard your teeth creaking."

Aibhan seemed to notice him for the first time and slithered forward into his personal space, causing our local escorts to shuffle away from him. "Will you compete in the Trial as well? You are most pleasing to the eye. I would enjoy seeing you covered in the blood of your opponents."

He cleared his throat and awkwardly stepped away before she could surround him with her tail. "Unfortunately, I must decline, this time. I am sure you will enjoy Eve's fights. She can be quite...dramatic."

I frowned at him.

Fanir let out a low chuckle and wiped the sweat from his brow with a faintly trembling hand.

Jacky perked up. "What about me? I could compete!"

Sam poked her in the side. "You'd end up fighting Eve for her puzzle band. Just sit this one out."

Adam cleared his throat. "Aibhan, do you know anything about the person who brought Eve's puzzle here?"

Aibhan looked Adam up and down. "No, much too scrawny," she muttered to herself before saying, more loudly, "It was a mortal woman with a power given to dreams and shadows. I know only that."

When Jacky started asking Aibhan about her powers, Fanir seemed to decide my team was entirely too comfortable with the situation. Interjecting himself into the conversation, he bowed once more to the goddess. "Thank you for your benevolence, mighty Aibhan. We will bother you no longer."

He and the local enforcers politely but forcefully herded my team away from Aibhan, only regaining a measure of calm once we had returned to the makeshift city streets.

Chapter 3

Back on the ground level of the tent Fanir had housed us in, I paced back and forth, my scales rippling in agitation. Because of my now-non-retractable claws, I couldn't clench my fists without stabbing myself, which irritated me even more.

The local enforcers had bent a considerable portion of their resources toward finding the thief, but I had my doubts about their usefulness. Ironically, this was one of the few times I would have preferred Earth's extensive and privacy-invading network of monitoring equipment.

Sam suggested we ask Queen Mardinest for reinforcements, but I already knew that wouldn't work. She was in a difficult political situation as it was, and I knew she'd never agree to us, one of the main sources of political goodwill coming her way, publicizing our moment of weakness to the Estreyan people.

Frustrating as it was, I agreed with that. Announcing what had happened wouldn't help me get my puzzle band back. It was already too late for that. It would just make me seem vulnerable, less awe-inspiring, and more like a mortal with weaknesses that could be exploited. Drawing attention to the attack might invite further such attempts. We needed to handle this with as little fanfare as possible.

Adam rolled a small throwing knife between his fingers. "Why would this thief have come after you, specifically? She couldn't have been under some delusion that you were an easy target. This could have ended in her death if things had gone differently."

I snorted. "Except I *was* an easy target. I couldn't even fight back once I realized what was happening. She could have killed me just as easily as stolen the puzzle band."

Gregor scowled at his hands. "That's a good point. Why didn't she just kill you?" He rolled his eyes. "Wait, no, that's stupid. If she killed you, it probably would have sparked a worldwide manhunt, and she would have had even less chance of getting away with it."

Torliam grimaced. "Still, it leads to a good question. *Why?* She knew who you were. Almost everyone knows about the Oracle's three gifts to you. Did she hope to sell it to a black market buyer? Anyone who successfully solved the puzzle would be stuck with a crown irreversibly attached to their head, and their ill deeds would be visible for all to see."

Adam shook his head. "Regardless of why she wanted it, what went wrong? She realized we were tracking it and decided to get rid of it, but was vindictive enough to make sure that if she couldn't have it, no one could?"

Sam cleared his throat. "Maybe she never planned to sell it. What if she wanted the puzzle band because it's an artifact of power strong enough to increase the size of the Bestowal? From what I've heard, Aibhan bases the Bestowal on how entertaining the Trial is, and how impressive the offerings are. That's why everyone keeps hinting that we should join the Trial."

I stopped pacing. "Sam's right. She asked me if I planned to join the Trial tournament. When I said no, she said she had already thought that would be my answer, and the drug kicked in. What if her goal was only to get me to join the Trial, and never actually had anything to do with the puzzle band?"

Adam's fingers moved faster, till the knife was little more

than a blur between them. "Why would they want that? I sincerely doubt they're so low on contestants and offerings that they had to do something this dangerous. There are plenty of other people who would have been a less dangerous target. Hell, they could have just *asked* other levels or countries for volunteers."

Kris fidgeted. "Maybe we're in danger? Should we ask for some more guards? If they're targeting Eve…"

Everyone turned to the entrance as the lead enforcer, who'd introduced himself as Henrik, strode through.

Henrik nodded his head in a perfunctory bow. "We have gone through our records, and it seems this theft may have followed a pattern. There have been a high number of unsolved thefts reported over the last month or so, with a handful of them involving drugging. A couple of those who were drugged reported hallucinations, or perhaps a Skill with effects similar to the things you experienced, Eve-Redding."

"So we have a lead," I said, hoping my sigh of relief wasn't too obvious.

He hesitated. "The other thefts have not provided any specific clues to the identity of the thief, per se. These things do happen, as I'm sure you understand. We were not aware of any possible connection between them until now. However, we are aware of the location of a local…apothecary. We have suspected him as a possible supplier of illegal substances, but there is not enough proof for an arrest, and he has refused to cooperate with us. Perhaps, if the godkiller were to pay him a visit, it would loosen his tongue?" Enforcer Henrik swallowed awkwardly as he awaited my reaction.

I sighed. "What are we waiting for? Let's go."

THE RUMORED ILLICIT SUBSTANCE DEALER, a man by the name of Kasimir, wasn't any happier to see me or my teammates than he was the enforcers escorting us. He had a moderately large tent away from the busiest areas of the city. Little cloth pockets filled with bottles and packets lined the walls, and more hung down from the tent's roof.

When we walked in, my team and the enforcers filling the little shop to capacity, Kasimir's eyes flicked quickly over us, and a scowl settled onto his wrinkled face. "This ought to be another fun story for the bars," he muttered, then raised his voice. "What do you want? If you're going to be crowding out my paying customers, you'd best buy something or make it quick."

The lead enforcer explained why we were there in a clipped, businesslike tone, his nose wrinkled in an unpleasant expression as he looked around the tent.

Kasimir spat on the floor. "Messing with the Trial, that's bad for all of us. I wouldn't involve myself in anything like that, so if you think I helped these people, you can turn around and walk out right now. I have nothing to say."

I could feel my lips twitching in an attempt to rise in a snarl.

The enforcers stiffened, but before their leader could respond, Sam placed a hand on his arm and stepped forward. "We don't think you were involved," he said, his Earth accent very noticeable when compared to the natives. "But we thought you might be able to help, because of your connections."

I shifted to the side, allowing Sam to take the spotlight. Unlike most of the team, his first response to a challenge wasn't aggression. Perhaps that would be useful here. And if kindness didn't work, Sam's other Skill, Black Sun, was a much more effective information-gathering method than standard threats or even torture.

"I'm sure you understand the implications of what the thief did. Aibhan almost cancelled the Trial when she heard of the stolen offering." Sam's voice was gentle, but unhesitating. "Eve agreed to participate in the Trial and win back her artifact instead of receiving it directly from Aibhan, and that is the only reason this level will still be receiving water before an additional three cycles have passed."

Kasimir paled. "And if the thieves are not caught, what will happen?"

Sam shook his head. "Who can say? Perhaps they will continue to steal, and it will not affect the Trial. Perhaps they will continue to give those offerings to Aibhan, and the goddess will decide stolen offerings are an offense strong enough to return them all and postpone the Trial. In any case, I think you can understand why it's good for all of us to find them and stop them."

"I was not involved with this, truly. What more is there I can do to help?"

I decided that was my cue. "You can help us find the source of the drug they used on me. This is not the first time it's been used to commit a crime. The local enforcers seem to believe this is within your capabilities."

Kasimir shot them a glare. "Well." He sucked on his teeth for a few seconds before continuing. "You have a sample? I'm not promising anything, but I do have a better idea what goes on around here than the incompetent bumblers that try to pass off as law enforcement."

"Watch it!" one of the enforcers muttered. Henrik stiffened, his frown growing even more oppressive.

Sam spoke again before the antagonism between Kasimir and the enforcers could escalate. "I have a sample, of sorts. I can recreate a version of the drug that was used, though it won't be exact."

Kasimir waved my teammate forward. He seemed quite interested when Sam secreted the drug via spitting into a jar, and avarice gleamed from his eyes. "You find yourself tired of all the hero shenanigans, you'd make a fine apothecary, boy. I've been in need of an assistant, you know. Pay's good, job's pretty much hassle-free except for the occasional idiot customer and the enforcers."

Gregor snorted and shot said enforcers an amused smile, seeming to take perverse pleasure in the old man's insults.

Sam cleared his throat awkwardly. "Err, thanks, but…"

Kasimir waved his hand to stop Sam from continuing. "Bah! No need to deny me now. Just keep it in mind."

Sam looked at me helplessly.

I shrugged at him.

Kasimir took about half an hour to examine the substance Sam had recreated, going so far as to catch a lizard and shove a swab of the hallucinogen in its mouth. It collapsed shortly afterward, its legs twitching faintly and its bulging eyes rolling around in distress.

Kasimir nodded sharply. "Well, it's about what I expected."

"What is it?" I asked, unable to keep the eagerness out of my voice.

"I cannot be sure since what hero-boy has given me isn't an exact match of what you took, and I've never examined the original, but it looks like a drug I've been hearing about accompanied by talk of a certain criminal group. Showed up a couple of moons ago. There's been some…*recreational* use of it, a couple of panic attacks and people coming to me thinking they're poisoned after taking it. I've heard rumors of thefts, too. People start seeing crazy things, they collapse, and while they're helpless, the gang robs all their valuables. But no one too important has been touched, so the enforcers couldn't be troubled to investigate."

Henrik flushed angrily under his tan. "We do not ignore our people, no matter their social standing. We had no *leads*. *You* refused to speak to us!"

Kasimir snorted, a sound that reminded me of Gregor, and ignored the man. "The group has some silly name like the Red Shadow or something like that. I can ask around for you, but, despite what these people seem to think, I do *not* have free access to the nefarious underground. I don't know what I can find out, and it might take a while."

I flexed my fingers, let out a silent breath, and nodded at Kasimir.

Adam laid a hand on my shoulder. "We'll keep looking, Eve. You just focus on the tournament."

Kasimir tapped his finger thoughtfully on his desk. "Perhaps you would like an antidote to this drug? In case you were to encounter these people again in your search."

Sam shook his head. "I can handle it if anyone gets dosed."

I frowned. "But what if you're not there at the time, Sam? It's very fast-acting."

"My antidote would negate the effects almost immediately," Kasimir piped up. "As they say, it is better to carry more water than you think you need."

"Make some," I said to Kasimir. "Torliam will pay you."

Torliam sighed deeply. "How did I become the purse-strings of this group?" he grumbled to himself as we left the tent.

"You've got access to the vaults," Adam shot back. "It's not like the money is coming out of your own pockets, so stop complaining."

Before they could continue bickering, Zed spoke up. "We need to keep a guard on Eve. We've been too lax. We don't know how dangerous these people might be."

I frowned. "Actually, I'm more worried about the puzzle band. They're *thieves*. We should check out these other stolen artifacts. See if they somehow ended up in Aibhan's Well. Maybe put a watch on it. Isn't it common for criminals to return to the scene of the crime?"

Jacky nodded emphatically, bouncing a little in excitement. "At least, that's what always happens in the films. So we're gonna lay an ambush to capture them?"

"Maybe. It's best to be prepared for any eventuality we can think of. Something feels…off about all this."

<hr>

Chapter 4

<hr>

Fanir found new, less vulnerable accommodations for us in a less fancy tent.

I asked Zed to let Blue, the Other Place sentience, know that I wouldn't be visiting to provide fire that evening due to extenuating circumstances. Since I spent the time pacing back and forth uselessly instead, I might as well have just made a dent in my enormous debt to Blue.

My teammates urged me to sleep and took turns keeping watch. It now seemed foolish to entrust our safety to our guard from the capital or any of the local enforcers. We could trust ourselves best.

The enforcers promised us that the travel restrictions out of the city would remain active, in hopes of finding the thieves if they tried to escape.

When morning came, I prepared to head to the Trial arena. Fanir had a hard time disguising his excitement. Apparently, he'd advertised my involvement in the Trial as widely as possible in the short time he had. It would have irritated me a lot more if I thought he was being nefarious rather than simply opportunistic.

Jacky, Sam, and the kiddos accompanied me to the arena.

People crowded around, lively in the cooler morning air. Vendors loudly advertised their wares, people ran around dressed up like warriors, and parents held children on their shoulders. It reminded me of the commotion surrounding the popular sports on Earth, except this was about more than entertainment.

Aibhan had raised and molded the ground around the outside of the arena into row upon row of coliseum style seating, creating a giant amphitheater from which to view the coming spectacle. Three cylinders jutted out of the ground of the arena itself, their smooth surfaces contrasting with the rest of the arena, which looked like a mix of burnt cottage cheese and coral.

The tallest of the three cylinders held Aibhan herself, and the other two, larger and closer to the ground, were empty. Those would be the fighting rings for the first day of the Trial.

The live area for the fights would increase the second day, and on the third day would include the entire arena.

Nothing fancy was required, Fanir had assured me, though it was preferred that the contestants put on a bit of a show rather than ruthlessly taking out their opponent before the full measure of a warrior's strength could be revealed.

Jacky jumped, letting her Skill help her float above the crowd as she looked down at the fighting rings. "It's just like mixed martial arts, like I used to do on the streets! I made good credits off those fights!" She pounded her fist into her hand excitedly. "I'm gonna go put some money on you. You better win!"

Gregor looked from Jacky, to me, then back to Jacky. "Good idea. Put some money on Eve for me, too!"

Sam groaned and palmed his face with his hand. "And now you've got the children gambling, Jacky. We're the *worst* influences."

Gregor rolled his eyes in a put-upon manner. "It's not like this is an actual *gamble*. I'm not *stupid*. Eve's going to win because she wants her puzzle-loop-thing back. When have you ever seen Eve lose when she really wants to win?"

I grimaced. I could think of more than a couple times. But I didn't say that out loud.

"I'm just making some extra spending money," Gregor said.

Sam shook his head. "You know, gambling addicts always believe they're going to win, too?"

While the two of them bickered, Jacky ran off to place the bets, and Kris shared a sympathetic look with me, resolutely ignoring the attention of the crowd as we passed through to the arena.

By the time the sun had risen fully over the horizon, the stands had filled with people.

Sam, Jacky, and the kiddos sat next to me and the other contestants at the bottom edge of the arena while we waited for things to start.

Despite my late entry, someone had inserted me into the tournament lineup smoothly. Two large scrolls of paper at the edge of the arena showed the matchups for each fighting ring. I didn't recognize the name attached to mine, but I wasn't concerned. This was all only a means to an end. After every-thing I'd gone through, being nervous about a fight was ridiculous.

At least, that's what I told myself to ease the tension building in my neck and shoulders.

After half an hour of increasing impatience, a local wearing brightly colored clothing and a wide-brimmed hat covered with little bells walked out into the arena, bowed to Aibhan, and turned to the crowd.

"Welcome, those from near and far! As is our tradition, we gather here today to witness the blood games in tribute to the Goddess Aibhan, who graces us with her presence and the waters of life!"

The cheer from the crowd was deafening and went on for longer than I thought reasonable.

The announcer hyped up the Trial for a few more minutes, and then the first two fights started. The first day was about whittling down the contestants to a more reasonable number, so each of us would fight twice. Only the winners continued on to the next fight, and from there to the next day of the Trial.

We munched on snacks Jacky had purchased from the nearby vendors and watched idly. Some fights were more impressive than others, and I took note of the winners and their abilities in case I ended up facing them.

When the announcer finally called my name, the crowd roared in excitement, stomping their feet on the stone stadium till the whole world seemed to tremble and vibrate with the collective force of it.

I went up to the closest stone ring and jumped atop it. I tuned everything out, regulating my breathing and the slightly too-fast beat of my heart.

Across from me stood a young man. He seemed nervous, and held a shimmering bow that glowed with power under Wraith's assessment.

We bowed to each other, and then the announcer called for a start to our fight.

My opponent sprang toward the side and away from me, covering half the ring in a single move.

My heartbeat thundered in my ears, and Chaos writhed just under my skin.

He drew back his glowing bow and an arrow of light shot toward me, faster than any primitive projectile had a right to move.

I would have been skewered through the stomach if I hadn't already been moving before he released the arrow. I dodged to the side with a small hop.

The archer disappeared, sucked into himself in a swirl of brightness that resembled a mid-air whirlpool. He reappeared to my side and slightly behind me, before my feet even fully regained purchase on the ground.

He drew back another arrow with blurring speed, but Chaos was faster. It burst from my skin as easily and quickly as popping a balloon with a needle. My power condensed as it went, forming midnight black, tendon-like cords of condensed Chaos, which lashed through the air with a deadly whistle.

I had to consciously temper my power when I hit him, letting the black cords branching out of the skin of my back unravel a little.

Still, the half-misty force that hit him in the torso broke the skin and probably cracked a couple ribs.

He crumpled to the ground.

I stepped forward to make sure I hadn't severely injured him and, of course, to force him to concede defeat with the threat of more injury.

Before I'd taken more than a couple steps, he'd done his little teleportation trick and was on the other side of the arena again. He held himself gracelessly, but the injury didn't seem to affect his ability to shoot his bow. This time, he shot three arrows at once.

I was forced to twist awkwardly while throwing myself to the ground. I landed chest-down on the stone and pushed up again immediately, my inhuman strength enough to literally throw my body back into the air.

While I was still righting myself and unable to maneuver properly, he shot three more arrows.

I gritted my teeth in frustration and let Chaos explode out of me, this time in a thick misty haze.

The light arrows didn't disintegrate when they touched it like I had hoped. Instead, they pierced through the cloud of Chaos like lightning through rain clouds. One scraped against the scales of my torso. It *burned*, and left behind a dark scar on the natural armor.

My opponent kept his bow trained vaguely toward me, but didn't shoot again. He was likely waiting to see if he'd managed to hit me through the artificial darkness.

I didn't bother dropping Chaos to let him find out. Instead, I slammed it outward in a single concussive wave, powering it with enough force to launch him off the fighting ring and down to the craggy, smoldering ground below.

It was my win.

The crowd cheered my victory, but the blood pounding in my ears and the pain from my side soured any satisfaction I might have felt. Chaos writhed around me like a pacing animal, resisting as I drew it back into my body and forced its dark currents to obey.

Even once I was back at the base of the stands with my teammates, high-fiving Jacky and ruffling Gregor's hair, I had trouble calming.

Sam made short work of the burned scales on my side, waving away the tournament-issued healer when she moved toward us. When he was done, he reactivated Black Sun. His eyes grew slightly shaded, and he wore a lazy grin on his face as he watched my opponent limp away from the arena under the care of two healers.

I caught a glimpse of his eyes, and my antsy energy settled a bit under the ambient weight of his power.

"Everything's still okay with the others," he said. We'd agreed that they wouldn't contact me through a Window unless it was an emergency, in case they distracted me while I was fighting. Sam was acting as a temporary liaison.

I nodded, then returned to brooding as I waited for my second fight. I'd been so stupid, getting myself into this situation in the first place. I wasn't invincible, and acting like I was was reckless and dangerous. Hell, I'd just been injured fighting against a single normal Estreyan, who wasn't even *that* powerful. Sure, I'd been trying to make sure I didn't kill him, but it shouldn't have happened.

My Resilience and Life were both pretty high, but…I was still kind of a glass cannon. I could do a lot of damage, but without Torliam and Adam to shield me, I probably would have been obliterated long ago.

Scratch that, I *definitely* would have been obliterated. I could think of a handful of times just off the top of my head that they'd shielded me from certain death. I'd just openly demonstrated my weakness, and it didn't feel good.

By the time the irritating announcer in his jingly hat called me up for my second fight, the sun was high in the sky, I was hungry again, and my irritation had built up into a low-level seething frustration. I focused on my opponent, a hulking muscle-bound man with a slightly protruding brow. I would do better this time.

As soon as the announcer started the fight, I swept my arm in a wide arc, and Chaos rushed out in a dark cloud to follow the motion.

The man flexed his muscles just as my attack impacted him, meeting it head-on.

I heard the screech of metal and the rumble of shaking stone under my feet, but the barbarian of a man stepped forward unharmed, his skin now a dull grey.

His footsteps were heavy enough to put hairline cracks in the stone beneath his feet, which meant whatever metallic substance he'd morphed into probably went all the way through his body.

I danced around him on my animalistic, clawed feet, testing his reaction speed.

Metal Man wasn't slow. Whatever bulk he had, he had the strength to match it, and it translated into a speed that made his fist whistle as it punched through the air toward me.

I dodged, suddenly grateful for the oversized ring that kept me from being forced into close proximity with Metal Man. Another wave of Chaos, and once again I heard the agonized screeching of metal as Chaos drove into him, but he barely even flinched.

Dodging and scampering around the ring as he came after me with single-minded focus, I increased the potency of my attacks, using a little more of the raging power inside me, hitting a little harder, condensing the dark mist a little thicker.

It wasn't till I noticed that some of the heat waves in the air were coming directly off his body, and he seemed to be moving even faster and more smoothly than before, that I realized my tactic might not be working.

In fact, it seemed to have done the opposite.

I fell back and simply evaded.

He grinned widely in response and nodded at me, as if to confirm that all my efforts had only been self-sabotage. "I absorb energy," he said simply, the words a rumble in the air. Then he shot forward, moving faster than he had the entire fight.

I was at the edge of the arena, so I jumped upward, clearing his head by a few feet as he arrived where I had been standing. I flipped in mid-air, preparing to land on my feet and knock him off the edge with a Chaos-infused kick to the back.

His arm reached behind his back, and, without even looking, he caught my foot in one massive hand, then wrenched.

The opposing force of his swing against my momentum pulled at my ankle, my knee, and my hip until they screamed out in agony from the unnatural force trying to rip them apart.

Metal Man swung me through the air, but instead of tossing me outward and down to the arena floor for an automatic disqualification, he spun around and smashed me into the ground of the raised ring.

I hit shoulder first, and a millisecond later my head smashed into the stone and bounced off. Stars burst behind my eyes and I lost track of the world for a moment.

Metal Man kept hold of my foot, but didn't attack further.

My vision spun horribly as my eyes began to function again, and I forcefully held back the vomit rising from my stomach. Wraith showed me only a confusing jumble of sensation that made me even dizzier. Had my skull cracked?

His hand shifted around my foot, and I panicked.

I convulsed against it, yanking my leg back and trying to wriggle out of his grip even as I attacked, my claws ripping at his sausage-like fingers and Chaos reaching toward him like a devouring maw.

I didn't hold back. I beat and tore at him, drilling inward and then ripping out. Chaos coalesced around us in a writhing cloud full of whips and thorns and teeth.

My foot was free for some time before I actually noticed. When I did, I scrambled backward.

Metal Man was lying on the ground in a fetal position, so I pulled back Chaos, letting it swirl and writhe around my body in little strands like prehensile hair.

The destruction shouldn't have surprised me, but somehow it did.

Half the ring was gone, torn or crumbled or melted away under the onslaught of Chaotic energy. Metal Man was centered in the worst of it and wasn't in much better shape. Melted slag had been spattered around, some of it molded like dough, as if hands had torn it away and squeezed before discarding it. Other injuries looked like worm-holes bored into and through him, and his right arm was completely missing from the elbow down, ending in a jagged and lumpy stump.

I stepped toward him hesitantly, the strands of condensed Chaos still floating around me. I guided a few strands into a larger, appendage-like shape and reached toward him, intending to poke him and make sure he was still alive.

He was, and he scrambled away desperately, clumsy with so many injuries and only three limbs. He let out a heaving, breathy sound that I only recognized as a sob from the look of pleading horror on his face as he crawled away from me.

I pulled back the tendrils of Chaos.

He bowed to me, pressing his forehead into the ground as he yelled a garbled word over and over. It was only when the announcer called my name as the winner of the fight that I realized he was yelling, "Forfeit."

I was self-aware enough to realize I'd overreacted.

My opponent could have won by disqualifying me, but instead chose to draw the fight out for the spectacle. He'd waited to make sure I wasn't seriously hurt when he slammed me into the ground. In return, I'd…done *that* to him.

I pulled Chaos in closer to my body, but instead of withdrawing the physical manifestation of my power, I pushed it toward the ground, wrapping the tendrils carefully around my damaged leg, fortifying it so I could walk. Already, the pain was fading somewhat as my Seeds rushed to fix the damage, but I was still no match for someone of Sam's abilities.

The medics were already rushing toward us, presumably to help Metal Man.

With barely a limp as Chaos supported me, I walked to the edge of the ring and prepared myself to jump off.

There was a distant cracking noise I recognized as gunfire, followed by a roar that reverberated through the air and stopped me in mid-stride.

I turned to look back up at Aibhan's main butte, the one that held her Well and the offerings for the Trial.

Panicked birds exploded up from the trees atop the goddess' lush abode.

A SERPENTINE FORM that held multiple people on its back and glittered like a rainbow curled up after the birds, sliding from tree to air like it was swimming. As it went, the red and orange in its coloring became more prominent, and it morphed into a flaming bird.

There were another couple *cracks* as Zed shot at them, but as far as I could tell he either wasn't hitting, which was unlikely for someone of his abilities, or his bullets weren't doing any actual damage.

An ink-black, gigantic, buzzing bee followed after the

flaming bird, but, despite its maneuverability, it couldn't keep up with the bird, which shot straight up toward the sun.

I squinted at it, reaching out with Wraith to see if the thief, who I'd dubbed Red in the absence of an actual name, was one of the riders.

I was blinded by the sudden flare of light that flashed out from the flaming bird, bright enough to obscure even the sun. When the spots passed from my eyes, the creature and its riders were gone not only from my sight, but to Wraith as well. It was as if they'd literally disappeared in the flash of light. Maybe they had. I'd dealt with one teleporter already that day, after all.

Damn aliens and their cop-out powers.

With a deep sigh, I sent a Window to the members of my team who'd been stationed secretly atop Aibhan's butte.

—Everyone okay?—
-Eve-

—Fine. Can't believe those bastards got away.—
-Zed-

The ground underneath me trembled as Aibhan snarled at the sun.

The other tournament fight had stopped, both contestants standing around with one eye on each other and the other eye awkwardly looking around for a hint about how to proceed.

My teammates appeared on the back of another ink construct, which skittered down the side of the butte and ran across the arena toward me without wasting any time.

The people in the stands, the other contestants, and the enforcers assigned as security had all realized that something was seriously wrong and were responding with varying levels of competence.

Aibhan turned to me, looking down from her pedestal. "I am displeased. Find them."

I nodded. That was the plan, after all. I jumped down off the platform, refusing to wince at the pain that flared out from my leg on impact with the smoldering ground below.

My teammates all converged on my location, and we crawled atop the centipede-like thing Adam had created.

I very carefully didn't look at it too hard. I'd never been afraid of bugs *before* Pestilence, and despite my subconscious screaming at me that the ink-form should be associated with mortal terror, I refused to give in.

Before Adam could set the bug steed to moving again, following whatever direction Torliam indicated, three familiar Estreyans hurried across the arena, weaving through the coral-like growths and squinting against the smoke to reach us before we left. "We will accompany you!" Henrik yelled.

Adam rolled his eyes. "Hurry up, then!"

The enforcers crawled up behind us, and we set off toward the city, Jacky letting out a battle cry and waving her arm around in a circle like some old-world cowgirl.

"How far?" I yelled.

Torliam turned back to look at me. "Toward the outer edge of the city. We must hurry. I have called our ship to meet us there, in case they attempt to escape again."

I grinned. Even if they did try to escape, Torliam had them now. We would be able to find them no matter where they went.

"How did you know they would return to the Well?" Henrik yelled in my ear, leaning forward behind me.

"Just a hunch!" I shrugged. It was the truth, but still… I glanced toward Zed and sent him a Window with a thought.

—Did they seem surprised to see you?—
-Eve-

Zed turned around to me and nodded.

—Completely.—

-Zed-

—And was there a redheaded woman?—
-Eve-

—I didn't see one. Unless she can change her appearance
at will, pretty sure she wasn't there.—
-Zed-

I frowned. Perhaps she'd simply been using whatever her Skill was to hide. It had made her disappear from my room, and, seeing as she was part of a semi-famous thief gang around here, I didn't want to discount the possibility of effective stealth Skills. I looked around warily, the hair on the back of my neck rising with the suspicion that we were being watched.

I turned my head back to Henrik. "The blockade of the city's exit routes is still up, right?"

He nodded to me, deeply enough that it was almost a bow, then had to catch himself as the ink construct jerked sharply around members of the alarmed crowd milling at the edge of the arena.

Torliam guided us to the eastern edge of the city, where the tents became increasingly strange in their layout, sometimes more than one fabric building stacked atop others like a weird Lego land built by incompetent children. Any semblance of an orderly road disappeared, and we wove through the pseudo-jungle so fast it reminded me of a theme park ride back on Earth.

The skyline above the silhouette of the surrounding tents flashed with light for a split second. My heart sank.

The muscles in Torliam's neck jumped as he ground his teeth together.

I kept Wraith on the lookout for any sign of our prey, but by the time we arrived in front of a particularly jumbled mass of tents, I already knew. I sent a message to the rest of the team.

—I don't feel anyone in there.—
-Eve-

Torliam threw himself off the ink construct and dashed through the closest doorway.

The rest of us scrambled to follow him.

Inside, the room was a mess. Furniture was overturned. Dishes were laid out, some with half-eaten food still warm atop them. "They left in a hurry," I murmured aloud. "They must have teleported away with that morphing firebird Skill again."

Torliam cursed, and a sky-blue mist swirled around him violently, kicking up a wind that whipped a few strands of loose hair across my face.

Jacky turned around and moved as if to punch the wall, but stopped herself just before hitting it. She clenched her fist and chuckled. "Better not. Might bring the whole thing down on our heads, no?"

Kris jumped down from her marionette's shoulders and walked to the door at the back of the room, which led into a hallway.

I already knew there was no one there, but I went with her just in case. We didn't know what all their Skills were yet. If someone popped out of the air and kidnapped her or something, I wouldn't be able to forgive myself. I'd already made one mistake in trusting the redhead to begin with. I wasn't going to make another mistake now.

Kris reached up one tiny hand and grabbed mine as we walked through the hallway, looking one by one into a series of individual rooms.

They, too, were disturbed and had obviously been left in a hurry.

We walked past a few open doors, but stopped in front of the fourth shabby room. The panic was evident in this one, too, but it wasn't the mess that drew my attention. It was the chain on the floor and the bars on the window. It was the covered bucket in the corner and the faint stench of urine that made my nose wrinkle. My heart grew cold and sank into my stomach.

I hadn't noticed any of this with Wraith. With all the mess, one ordinary object without Seed glow was similar to any another, and I'd been more focused on the broad picture than picking up little details.

Kris' fingers tightened around my own. "Is that…"

I gripped her hand harder in response. "Yeah." Quickly, I tugged her to the door of the next room and found a similar setup. There were drawings on the wall that looked like they might have been done by a child, and there was a wooden doll discarded on the floor beneath the barred window.

I found myself breathing fast. I pulled Kris to the next door and found another room with chains, this time a set, with a bar connecting the two shackled ends. It would go between someone's arms or feet to keep their limbs spread and impede movement.

Kris moved as if to step into the room, but I held her back. "This is a crime scene. We can't disturb it," I said.

She drew her lips into an exaggerated grimace. "Torliam can find them, right? Even if they ran away before we got here? 'Cause the evidence is disappearing." She pointed to the chains and drew my attention back to them.

They were disintegrating. I focused Wraith on them immediately, and found that they weren't simply turning to dust, but disappearing as if they'd never existed. With a curse, I screamed out, "Torliam! Get here right now!"

He rushed around the corner with superhuman speed, stopping beside Kris and me, misty blue energy already glowing from his raised fists. He looked over us with concern and then around us for a threat.

"There's no danger, but the evidence is already evaporating," I explained quickly, motioning him toward the chains on the floor and the bars on the window opening. "Take in as much as you can. Maybe you can find them if they do it again."

Torliam looked, but within seconds the last of the evidence, except for the bucket of human waste in the corner, was gone.

The rest of the team and the enforcers hurried around the corner but were too late to see. Still, the half-filled, stinking buckets were enough to prove we were telling the truth.

As the enforcers searched through the various rooms, Torliam rubbed his face, his frustration obvious. "My sense of the thieves who approached the Well is muted. They must have some idea of my Tracker Skill, to place themselves under wards strong enough to hinder it."

Adam raised his eyebrows and scoffed in anger, half turning away. "Is that seriously enough to stop you? A simple security device?"

Torliam scowled at him. "'Simple' is not the word I would use to describe something capable of obstructing my Skill. It is likely they are using an artifact of great power. However, *I* found the lost god. Of course it is not enough to stop me. It will simply take more time."

"Time we can't afford to waste!" Adam snapped.

I held up my hands to stop them bickering further. Seriously, they could be like children sometimes.

Sam glared into the room that had held the doll and the scribbles on the wall, an aura of coldness radiating off him in my mind's eye. "Child trafficking?" he asked.

One of the enforcers met his gaze and jumped like a frightened rabbit, looking away and focusing on the wall with conspicuous focus. "Well…yes, it seems like it. Or perhaps they had them captured for some other reason. From what we've been able to dig up, these people call themselves the Crimson Shadows, and they don't limit themselves to simple thievery. Well, if you count organ theft and resale as thievery, then maybe they do? What I mean is, blackmail is not uncommon among groups like this."

Gregor hadn't stopped scowling since we arrived. "Is there any way for you to find out who might be being blackmailed?"

The enforcer rubbed the back of his head awkwardly, looking at Gregor while carefully avoiding Sam's gaze. "Maybe we can find a clue they left behind in their hurry?"

Gregor rolled his eyes and turned to me as if pleading for me to understand his frustration.

I sighed and shrugged. I wanted to say something to him, but I wasn't sure what.

Gregor sneered at the enforcer and moved to stand by me and his sister. He leaned down to let Kris climb atop his shoulders, and I realized that the boy had grown since I'd met him. He still barely came up to my waist, but then again…I'd grown, too.

I flexed my toes against the ground, making little rips in the fabric of the tent floor with my claws.

Jacky noticed, moving next to me and bumping me with her shoulder. "Let's go outside while the enforcers finish examining things, yeah? We're not gonna find anything here, anyway."

I knew she was right. I'd already used Wraith to go over every room in detail, and I hadn't found anything resembling a clue that would aid our search. If something was going to be found, we wouldn't be the ones to do it.

We filtered outside with a sigh, and the locals who'd been peeking out of their doorways, windows, and around the corners of nearby buildings perked up with greedy fascination. It was night by then, and the last few hours had held nothing but frustration.

Adam grumbled and spilled out a large cartridge of ink onto the ground, letting it form into a huge bird as it splashed. We climbed atop it, and he flew us away with a great heave of black wings.

Chapter 5

The next morning, the second round of the Trials started. This time, the twenty-five remaining candidates were divided into three groups, and each group would fight in a free-for-all within a section of the main arena. After that, the three semifinalists, one from each group, would compete the next day, and the one who came out on top would be the ultimate champion.

Obviously, since the number of contestants didn't divide evenly into three, there were two groups with eight, and one with nine. My group had that extra person, which Fanir had explained was because I was the one polling highest to win out of all the current contestants.

There'd also been some talk about marketing potential, what with me being "one of the Nine."

As I sat at the edge of the stadium seating, I got more than a few dirty looks from the other contestants.

Jacky cracked her knuckles. "Think these things ever break out into a fight before the actual Trial starts? They've got us all grouped up together, someone might decide to take out the competition when they're not expecting it. Of course..." She laughed with a cocky smirk. "If they try something, I'm gonna smash them into the ground so hard people won't be able to get the dirt out of their chunky bits."

I stared at her blankly for a few moments, then sputtered out a laugh. "Their *chunky bits?*"

Her grin melted into a sullen pout. "Yeah, that's right! Don't make fun of me." She poked out a finger and dug it into my side.

I wriggled to get away from her, unable to hold back my laughter.

"Where is their respect for this competition?" One of the other contestants said, loudly enough it was obvious they wanted us to hear. "Does she feel so cocky that she was picked for the nine-person group that she looks down on the rest of us?"

One of the others, a large man with muscles even bigger than Torliam's, leaned back and crossed his arms over his chest. "'Godkiller' is just a title the stupid masses have given her. She is not one of us. She has no right to act like she is better than us. I will teach her to be more humble when I crush her under my heel."

Another person laughed. "You go ahead and do that. And then I will knock you unconscious and take the final prize for myself."

I held back a sneer.

Gregor leaned forward to look at my expression with a frown on his face. "You're not going to lose, right?"

"Of course not."

"But…you got hurt yesterday, and it was only the first round. These people won all their fights, too."

I bit the inside of my lip, then released it and tried to look nonchalant. "I barely got hurt. And that's because I was holding back. I didn't want to hurt any of them too badly until I knew how much damage they could take. I could have won with one hit if I was being serious."

Gregor leaned back and shared a look with Kris. "She's a braggart."

I just couldn't win. First, he was worried I was going to lose and now he complained I was too egotistic?

Kris giggled and turned to grin at me, swinging her legs off the edge of her seat. "It's okay if you want to brag a lot, Eve. Just make sure to win. I made a bet on you, so you better not make me lose all my candy money."

My mouth dropped open. "You're gambling, too?!"

Kris simply nodded. "Yeah."

I dropped my head into my hands, my claws scraping against my scalp. "Blaine would kill me if he heard about this. How is it that, despite my best efforts, his niece and nephew have turned into a couple of little gamblers? What's next? Blackjack and hard alcohol?"

Kris patted me on the back. "It's okay, just blame it on Jacky."

I just groaned into my hands, playing it up for the kids' amusement. Before I could continue the conversation, though, the call for the first group to enter the arena echoed through the stands.

Nine of us converged on the arena floor. Once we were there, Aibhan waved her hand and the ground shifted under our feet, carrying each of us off in a different direction. She would place us randomly around the battlefield.

Tiny aerial cameras captured the arena from above and displayed us on large screens. The screens were placed so that we couldn't use them to help ourselves find opponents, but all the spectators would be able to get a clear view of the free-for-all fight.

The announcer with the stupid hat took his sweet time yammering, hyping up each contestant while we stood around and waited. When he finally started the fight, I'd already gotten the location of all my opponents and the layout of the section of the arena we were limited to.

I was still irritated over the events of the last few days, and I have to admit I was looking forward to the fight. I needed a chance to release some frustration. I had no plans to start out as softly as I had the day before. All these contestants had fought and won twice to be here, so they shouldn't have a problem taking a hit from me.

I walked calmly through the maze-like, smoking protrusions, hopping over the places where the ground would collapse into a mass of glowing heat if stepped on and avoiding the deep fissures. The ground was roasting under my bare feet, and I was grateful for the toughness of the skin there.

I once again lamented the lack of a second, semi-transparent eyelid. Without Wraith, the smoke likely would have obscured my vision to the point of tears and made things much more difficult.

I'd only made it a few meters when the sound of an explosion blew past and the ground rumbled under my feet. One of the contestants, whose Skill created concussive blasts strong enough to shatter stone, had just taken out another contestant.

I let Chaos bubble out of my skin, gathering a thick mist of it around me.

All the contestants were converging on the middle, some more directly than others.

I stepped forward around the corner of one particularly large protrusion, and a neon green beam cut through the mist of Chaos in front of me.

I'd known they were there, of course, along with the *other* contestants hiding against the opposite side of the small clearing under a covering of light grey ash.

It was mostly happy coincidence that the instinctive attack by the green blaster hit the person hiding instead of me.

I couldn't have arranged it better if I planned it.

My eyes widened as I observed the effects of said beam. Everything it touched turned green to match, as the target was converted into a tightly packed mass of spring-fresh leaves.

The announcer loudly called out the victim's elimination from the Trial.

I grimaced. Well, I probably shouldn't have provoked that attack. I hadn't meant to get the hidden person *killed*.

With a flash of power, I sent a rolling wave of Chaos straight through the mass of coal and earth separating me and Mr. Green Beam.

He tried to dodge, but Chaos spread out like a pincer and closed in on him. He wasn't fast enough to evade that, too, and went down with an agonized scream as my power rippled through him and threatened to pull him apart.

A few seconds later, his name was called by the announcer. Mr. Green Beam wasn't dead, but he wasn't a threat to me anymore, either.

I flashed a small smirk to the camera I knew was focusing on me and continued on. Three of the other contestants met a few hundred meters away and immediately began a flashy battle, one throwing lava whips pulled from the fire beneath the ground, one flying, and one attacking with superhuman-level martial arts. Hopefully, they'd just take each other out.

A woman with crystalline armor and a glittering blade in each hand stepped around a bend and blocked my way, her stance an obvious challenge. Even a couple meters away, the cold from the ice she controlled was palpable against my skin.

I let Chaos roll forward again, and she stepped forward to meet it.

Her armor immediately grew thicker by a few inches, and though it shattered under the effects of my power, she made it through the cloud mostly unscathed. The armor and double blades reformed around her almost immediately.

I couldn't help but grin as I sidestepped around a swing of one knife and drove a clawed hand into her abdomen, crushing through the ice armor and digging into the skin below.

Before I could do any real damage, she'd twisted away, and I had to lunge back to avoid the other knife.

A spike of ice grew from the ground underneath me, and I crushed it with Chaos, then lashed out again, this time with cords instead of a mist, letting them branch out around her and then snap inward like the jaws of a trap.

She tried to guard with a wall of ice, but there were too many condensed strands of Chaos to leave any room for her to escape, and her Skill was no match for mine.

As Chaos crushed her defenses and began to bite into her skin, she screamed out, "Forfeit! Forfeit!"

I stilled, and Chaos stilled with me as I waited for the announcer to accept her disqualification, absently noting that the trio of fighters on the other end of the arena seemed to have broken up, but only one of them had been downed.

The person who could fire concussive blasts was shooting them about freely, taking down the obstacles in his path rather than going around them.

Once the ice user was officially withdrawn from the tournament, I withdrew the pulsing black strands slowly, allowing her to slump to the ground. None of her wounds were severe enough to be a real danger.

She glared at me, but then seemed to relax with a put-upon sigh. "Well, hurry up, then. Go knock the rest of them out so I can get to a healer before I die from the heat."

Something about her rude expression reminded me of Gregor, and it put a wry smile on my face as I turned to stop the surprise attack of the Estreyan who had been creeping up on us as we fought.

He sprang forward on all fours, his face twisted in an animal snarl and his sharp teeth dripping with saliva. Veins and tendons stood out from his skin, which seemed weirdly thin, and his muscles bunched just under the surface with a definition that bordered on the absurd.

I bent all the way backward and flipped over to avoid his attack, a move I couldn't have begun to attempt before I'd been enhanced with Seeds.

But he was faster than me. Much faster.

By the time I righted myself, he'd jumped off another coral-like protrusion and launched himself toward me again.

His problem was, he was only flesh and blood. Even if my body couldn't move as fast as his, my mind wasn't so limited.

Chaos came together in a shield-like wall and spiked toward him.

His skin burst and the bones broke where it touched, but before I could finish him off, I had to dodge the flying Estreyan's dive attack at my back.

A lava whip tried to intercept me, and I probably would have been sheared in half if I hadn't smashed a wave of Chaos into it in time. As it was, a few drops still splattered over me, sizzling atop my scales and burning the flesh beneath. Chaos, or at least my current grasp of it, wasn't very suited to shielding.

They were ganging up on me.

Wraith caught the movement of the half-animal man returning to attack again.

At the same time, the flyer maneuvered around to do the same.

Mr. Lava Whip motioned with his hands as if tugging and brought another glowing whip burrowing out of the ground below.

Mr. Concussive Blasts had almost finished bulldozing his way directly through the arena toward us.

The pressure was on.

I took a deep breath and closed my eyes as my foot touched the ground again. On the exhale, I lashed out with Chaos, condensed cords of power branching out toward each of the targets, moving so fast a human wouldn't have been able to catch it with their eyes.

A few strands latched around the legs of the flyer and slammed her out of the sky, cracking her into the ground hard enough to knock her unconscious.

More pierced through the lumped-up earth around us and

coiled around Mr. Concussive Blast's arms. A simple twist was enough to break them, which I hoped would make it too painful for him to continue using his Skill.

Thicker strands attacked the animalistic Estreyan, doing as much damage to his limbs as possible while simultaneously smashing him out of the air to crash into the growth dozens of yards away. Unless he had a significant healing factor, he'd need a medic to walk again.

A thin blade of Chaos sheared off the lava whip at its base. Before Mr. Lava Whip could summon another, the dark energy took his legs out from under him, but caught him as he fell. Taking a move out of my second opponent from the day before's playbook, I smashed him down to the ground with a crunch.

I regained my balance, looking around again as the dust settled.

Mr. Concussive Blasts was screaming in pain. Mr. Lava Whip seemed to be unconscious. Half-Animal was moaning to himself, drool running from his mouth where it was pressed into the ground. The flyer was also unconscious.

Miss Ice Armor was still sitting on the ground, now staring up at me in shock.

There was a beat of silence as the smoke swirled about with headache-inducing intensity, and then the jingling announcer screamed out my victory.

I only then realized I was grinning broadly, and relaxed my facial expression. My heart pounded, and the adrenaline rush left me feeling giddy. "That was close," I muttered to myself. If even one more opponent had ganged up on me at that time, I probably would have been defeated.

As I made my way slowly back to the seats where half my teammates waited, the crowd roared and stomped with enough fervor to shake both the air and the ground.

The giddiness followed me all the way back to my seat, and as I sat there, accepting the congratulations of my team and joking around with them, it mellowed out into a relaxation I hadn't felt for a while. I felt...*good.*

I wasn't stupid. I realized what that meant. I'd been so angry, after Pestilence. Even once we'd destroyed him, the anger hadn't gone away. I was pretty sure it wasn't *going* to go away. Something inside me had twisted, maybe broke. This feeling was only a temporary release, and, like an addict, I would need more. I could feel the anger waiting at the edges of my consciousness like a looming fog temporarily blown away by a breeze. It would roll back in. If I kept chasing the release, one day the danger would catch up to me, and I would *lose.*

It's not that I didn't care. It's just that I couldn't bring myself to care *right then.*

I STAYED to watch the second round, but by the time the third fight started, I found myself famished.

—ANY UPDATES?—
-EVE-

I sent the message to Zed, Torliam, and Adam, who were again secretly guarding Aibhan's Well while the other half of the team stayed with me. The members of our team at the Well could still oversee the arena and get to me quickly if needed, as they had the day before. The Crimson Shadows had tried to sneak up to the Well while everyone else was distracted by the Trial, and we had no idea if they would try again.

—NOTHING TO REPORT. WE'VE HAD TO EXIT THE OTHER PLACE A FEW TIMES TO WARM UP, BUT WE WERE CAREFUL NOT TO BE NOTICED, AND THERE'S NO SIGN OF THEM. I DOUBT THEY'RE GOING TO TRY THE SAME TRICK A SECOND TIME, SO I'M PRETTY SURE WE'RE WASTING OUR TIME. —

-ZED-

Before I could respond, he sent another message.

—ON THE OTHER HAND, BLUE ACTUALLY TALKED TO ME FOR A BIT EARLIER! HE WAS RUDE, BUT AT LEAST HE DIDN'T THREATEN TO KILL ME THIS TIME.——
-ZED-

I responded with a small smile, even though I knew Zed couldn't see it. Blue had been angry when Pestilence's death destroyed the Other Place. The huge whale-like creature had been slowly building the copy of reality up for what must have been almost an eternity, and had lost everything in the span of a few moments.

Sam, Jacky, and the kiddos stayed to watch the fight while I went to find a bucket load of food from the nearby street vendors.

Jacky asked if I wanted her to escort me, but she was so gleefully focused on the fight, I knew she didn't really want to. After my own fight, I didn't really feel like much could threaten me, anyway. I wouldn't accept any food or drink from strange redheads, so I should be fine.

Of course, it seemed like that thought had tempted the gods of irony.

Just as I was accepting a dozen spit-roasted lizards from a nearby vendor, I caught a flash of red hair from the corner of my eye.

My head snapped toward the side even as Wraith snapped toward the woman.

It was Red. She glanced toward me, green eyes just peeking past a lock of hair. Then she turned and walked around the street corner. As soon as she left my line of sight, she murmured into the air, "Call anyone, and you'll never see me again. Just you and me, and I'll let you catch up."

I felt a dark desire to burst out laughing like a crazy person in the middle of the street. I almost did as she said. Almost. Instead, I suppressed my reckless urges and sent a message to the rest of the team.

—I FOUND RED. OR RATHER, SHE FOUND ME. I THINK SHE WANTS TO TALK. SHE THREATENED TO DISAPPEAR IF I DIDN'T COME ALONE. BACKUP STAYS IN THE OTHER PLACE UNLESS I SIGNAL OTHERWISE. LEAVE SOMEONE AT AIBHAN'S WELL IN CASE THIS IS A DISTRACTION.—
-EVE-

—DO NOT SPEAK TO HER ALONE, EVE. THIS IS A TRAP.—
-ADAM-

I took a huge bite out of a roasted lizard and followed Red around the corner, sending a minimap Window to my teammates so they could follow me.

Red led me to a small out-of-the-way area between two tents, turning to face me as I arrived. "Congratulations on your win. After tomorrow, you will have your sparkly chain back and your life can return to normal." Her eyes drifted to an empty spot of air. Or at least, it was empty to all *my* senses.

I barely stopped myself from scoffing. "Congratulations? Funny, since you got me into all this." I couldn't help myself from following her gaze, remembering those negative-photograph fantastical creatures I'd seen when she'd drugged me. Were they there, even now, simply invisible to me?

She nodded, a small smile wrinkling the corner of her eyelids. "Are you complaining? From what I could see, you have been enjoying this. I do not believe you have had enough fighting for a lifetime, after all." She looked into the distance, then wrapped her arms around her torso as if she were cold. "I needed your involvement, your attention, and your interest. I did what I had to do." She looked up and met my eyes deliberately. "Do you understand?"

I remembered the chains. "It's hard to believe there was no better way to go about this."

She shook her head, squeezing herself tighter. "I cannot speak of it. Do you understand?" Each word was slow and deliberate, an obvious message beneath the surface.

I hesitated, but finally said, "Yes."

She seemed to deflate like a punctured balloon, but straightened again quickly. "Tomorrow, during the final fight. If one way is blocked, a determined individual will attempt another. Smoke obscures so much, especially when one's attention is focused on the stars within it. There will be a chance. The only chance to get *all* the pieces off the board in a single swipe." Her breath grew labored as she talked, and she leaned over as if dizzy. "The *only* chance I have been able to find, where the most *important* pieces are not destroyed."

I considered her words for a while, then gave her a single nod. Even if she were lying, Torliam had the mark of some of their other members now. It might take him a while, but they'd never be able to truly escape. I didn't have much to lose by going along with her, and there was a lot to gain.

Red met my eyes again. "Time is up, I think. You do not follow instructions well." She took a step backward into the shadow of a tent, and, with a flicker like static on a black-and-white television, disappeared.

Chapter 6

I stood watching the spot Red had been in, tapping my claws against my thighs as I replayed our conversation in my mind.

—Looks like she's gone. Safe for us to come out now?—
-Zed-

I nodded absently.

"Roger!" my brother said cheerily, ripping reality apart with his bare hands and stepping through.

Jacky and Torliam followed.

Torliam turned to me and stared silently for a moment. "You are very stupid," he said finally.

Zed and Jacky both seemed to agree with him, though they avoided looking me in the eyes while they nodded and grumbled.

"I was on my guard this time," I said. "And I learned something valuable."

Torliam rubbed his face. "Just because the result was acceptable, do you think your actions were acceptable, too? If you shoot an arrow at someone and by coincidence do not hit them, were you justified to shoot them?"

I flexed my fingers. "It was fine. This was an opportunity, and it paid off. If she'd tried anything, I would have killed her immediately. Let's focus on what she told me, instead. I don't think this has been a coincidence. Any of it."

Torliam clenched his teeth and growled, turning and stomping away a few dozen meters to seethe. When he returned, we moved to join up with the rest of our teammates while I related my conversation with Red to the three of them.

After the fights were over, Aibhan returned to her Well, and the whole team met up with the local enforcers.

Henrik bowed to me and began speaking immediately. "We have searched through our records for reports of those who have gone missing, working through the night to discover who may have been captured by the Crimson Shadows."

"And?" I said impatiently.

"We have compiled a list of suspected victims, though nothing sure. Their Skills seem quite suited to subterfuge and deception. However, we were able to assemble a profile of some of the Crimson Shadows' members, as well as some clues about their operational methods."

He handed me his datapad, and I read through the information quickly.

"I understand…" He tilted forward in what seemed to be an unconscious, apprehensive bow, "that you were contacted by the same member again?"

Torliam, his arms crossed and a glower on his face, nodded in answer.

"She was cryptic," I said. "She seemed to be under the effect of some Skill that disallowed her from talking freely about the Crimson Shadows. However, I believe they will be going after the Well again during the final round of the Trial tournament, tomorrow."

For once, Adam shared a commiserating look with Torliam. "You can't believe anything she said, Eve!"

Torliam said, "I will have their location pinpointed before

the sun rises again. We can move on them before they have a chance to complete whatever nefarious scheme they have planned."

Kris worried at her bottom lip and looked up at me. "What about the kids? I mean, at least one of them is a kid. What if we attack wherever they're hiding and the kidnappers decide to hold them hostage or hurt them?"

"My Skill will make it easy to save the kids first," Zed said. "We can do that before they even know we're there."

I remembered Red's cryptic words. Even if the other woman thought the only chance to capture the members of the Crimson Shadows while saving the captives at the same time was during the Trial's final battle, that didn't mean she was *right*. Basic information about my team's Skills was known to the public, but she might not understand the implications or the nuance of what we could do.

She could also simply be lying, holding the captives hostage in a more subtle way to try and give the Crimson Shadows a chance to escape.

Except, that brought me back around to the fact that I didn't believe they *could* escape. Torliam had them in the grips of his Skill. Even if they literally hid in another dimension, Torliam would eventually find them and lead us there.

So the question of what to do was really all about what would be safest for the people kept chained in those little rooms with the barred windows.

Attacking during the night would take the Crimson Shadows off guard, and we could probably save the captives before the others had a chance to threaten them. On the other hand, Red seemed to believe that wouldn't work, and she knew the capabilities of the Crimson Shadows' members better than we did. The information the enforcers had managed to gather was limited, and focused only on the higher-profile members, though we knew the Crimson Shadows had more than just them.

If we waited for the Crimson Shadows to carry through on

their plan, we'd have to deal with them while they were on guard. But if they left the captives behind while doing so, it would be easier for us to save said captives.

I resisted the urge to pace. Such an outward display of uncertainty wouldn't inspire confidence in anyone.

Really, the answer came down to how much I trusted Red. Which shouldn't have been much, based on simple logic. Except… if she was really on the side of the Crimson Shadows, stealing my puzzle band would have been the stupidest thing she could do. She'd drawn my attention to them and the Trial deliberately. She was using me, manipulating me. That was obvious.

But I wasn't so sure I wanted to stop her.

"We wait," I said, continuing before the others could protest. "The answer to problems like this never really changes. All we have to do is *win*. Also, we should probably talk to Aibhan again."

AS I WAITED for the final round of the Trial, I ran through a mental checklist of our preparations.

The enforcers were in place around the arena, both overtly as Trial security, and stationed in plainclothes throughout the crowd, hoping to go unnoticed by any assault force.

I didn't think they'd be much help if things went less than optimally, but any advantage was important.

"Any sign of 'em?" Jacky said, looking around surreptitiously.

Torliam responded in my stead. "They have not moved yet. I suspect they will not, until all eyes are focused on the spectacle within the arena."

I nodded and turned to look at Aibhan, who was coiled atop a tall column of smoking stone within the coliseum. She would watch the fight from there, as she had done the first two rounds.

The giant, half-snake woman met my gaze for a split second.

We both looked away.

My team was in place. Zed, Birch, and Adam guarded the offering-filled Well at the top of Aibhan's butte.

Jacky, Torliam, and Sam were with the kiddos and me.

I let my hand fall to the small pouch strapped to my leg and fingered the vial of antidote to Red's drug, which we'd picked up from Kasimir the night before. Just in case.

As the Trial announcer began to speak to the crowd, Wraith washed over my two opponents, taking stock of them without notice. Unlike the previous two days, I was taking this fight incredibly seriously from the beginning. I'd researched my opponents as well as I could, and I planned to attack with extreme prejudice. This was no longer a fight just for myself. If I slacked off here, I made things more dangerous for those the Crimson Shadows had captured, at least one of whom was a young child.

I flexed my muscles, and my scales rippled. I looked down at the alien changes to my body, from the glowing crystal at my throat, the scales and claws protruding from my flesh, to the inhuman, predatory shape of my feet. The corner of my mouth quirked up in the hint of a smile. I still had enough humanity left to care about the life of a child, at least.

My two final opponents were a horrible match for me, and not in my favor. Chaos was powerful, but their Skills had been enough to get them to the final round, too.

The woman, dark-skinned and a little shorter than me, was a self-regenerator, though there were hints that her power was a bit more complicated than that.

I was suitably wary.

The man, whose cheeks were pocked as if someone had extinguished a few cigarettes on his face, had an esoteric Skill that allowed him to alter and control the flow of energy from one form into another, turning fire into electricity, water into ice, and pretty much anything else you could think of.

As the announcer introduced us, we approached the arena. The crowd cheered, waved, and tossed tokens of appreciation at us, while the enforcers ensured none of them got too excited and tried to rush us physically.

Since I'd become known as the godkiller and destroyed Pestilence, it was not uncommon to command the attention of all those I met. It was irritating, but a stony glare into the distance was usually enough to dissuade even the most fervent of fans and the occasional critic, except it didn't *always* work. The crowd pressed toward us, pushing against the enforcers and the flimsy barricade bordering the path to the arena.

At least I had it better than the rest of my team, who seemed to come off as more approachable than me.

I ignored the dark stares of both my opponents, already planning my strategy.

This time, the entire arena was open to us. We could hide from and sneak up on each other, or even lead our opponents on a merry chase. The fight was supposed to be more dramatic and drawn-out than the first two, and all eyes would be on the combatants.

I sent Wraith out, surging against the edges of my range, looking for any signs of the Crimson Shadows or Red.

I twitched, but resisted the urge to jerk around as Wraith found her in the crowd, just one of the many reaching hands clawing at the combatants, hoping for just a touch, that brief moment of contact that they would tell their friends about for the next three years.

I wouldn't have been able to see her face even if I had looked, as it was covered by a low hood.

She lunged forward, breaking past the cordon of enforcers and grasping my hand with her own. Her palm was moist and a little sticky.

As the enforcers yanked her away from me, her bright green eyes met my icy gaze. Her expression was inscrutable, but I thought I caught a hint of desperation, or maybe it was guilt.

I let out a shuddering breath of horror as I looked down to my hand, where the sticky substance was already half-absorbed.

I frantically rubbed it off onto my clothing, knowing that it was too late to stop the reaction.

Adam had seen what happened and was rallying my teammates to capture her.

My two opponents and I stepped into the arena, and, as she had last time, Aibhan moved the earth under our feet to deposit us on opposite sides of the circular arena.

Behind me, Red disappeared into the crowd.

Chapter 7

I palmed the antidote in the pouch on my hip, feeling the vial inside. Kasimir had warned me that, though it would work almost instantly, the antidote had a short active duration and some debilitating side effects once it wore off. I only had about fifteen minutes, after which I would need to find a healer immediately if I wanted to continue functioning.

I took my hand away from the pouch as the announcer kicked off the final round of the Trial tournament. Whatever Red had done wasn't hitting me yet. Unlike the drug she'd given me in the water, this wasn't instant. It was even possible she'd dosed me with a completely different drug, though I suspected the side effects simply took longer to activate when it was being absorbed through the skin.

I would wait till the symptoms appeared to take the antidote. If it burned through the fifteen-minute time limit before the Trial was over and we'd defeated the Crimson Shadows, I'd be chopping off my own nose, so to speak.

I kicked myself for my stupidity. I'd based my choices on a feeling, some vague hunch that I could trust the redhead. My only consolation was that Torliam would have known if they'd used the extra time she bought to escape the city, so that hadn't been her ploy.

—Do you need me to come get you? Or maybe we can suspend this fight for a few minutes? You're not expected to start the fight injured. I'm sure we can make Aibhan understand.—
-Sam-

I doubted that was the case. The Trial had begun. Maybe we could have delayed if we'd been faster to act, but instead I had marched along in shock, spinning my mental wheels.

—I can still win this. Just wait. And keep your eyes peeled. Trouble is coming.—
-Eve-

Had everything from Red been a trick, then? But *why?* Killing me would have been much easier than this, if that's what they wanted. However, if she'd really been mostly on my side and merely in need of my help, why do *this?*

I flexed my tainted hand into a fist and started off through the arena, heading straight for the female regenerator. She would be the easier of my two opponents, I thought, and I couldn't risk both of them teaming up against me, not with my imminent handicap and what was at stake.

I had to get through this quickly. The faint wobble preceding the dizziness already pulled at my body.

The female finalist's eyes widened in surprise when she saw me approach, less than two minutes after the fight had begun.

Without a word, without hesitation, I let Chaos sweep out of me in a roiling cloud of darkness, pouring power into it until it condensed into a tangible shroud around me.

I attacked.

Chaos followed me, lending a terrible purpose to my movements.

My clawed hand smashed into her defending forearm, ripping and tearing. Chaos mimicked me, cracking through flesh and bone and continuing on down the arm toward the chest in a flurry of destruction.

I stopped when her chest collapsed under my onslaught. If she was anywhere near as good a healer as Sam, she would live. If not, I could probably volunteer his services to ensure she wasn't permanently crippled.

She buckled from the force of the blow with a scream that petered off as part of her ribcage cracked apart. Even Sam would need a few hours to heal from that.

I turned to walk away from her prone form, but the sounds of snapping bone stopped me. I turned back to her, watching with a sinking feeling as her wounds healed. No, not healed.

Disappeared. It was like watching a video in reverse. Even the blood splattered on her body disappeared, flowing back into her wounds before the skin sealed up. I noted that the splashes of blood that had hit the ground and soaked into the ash remained, unaffected by whatever her Skill actually was.

I narrowed my eyes as I watched her.

The last of her injuries vanished, and she turned to me with a threateningly blank look, like some kind of robot from a film.

She lunged toward me, faster even than Jacky could move, faster than I could dodge or create a solid shield. She smashed her fist into the center of my chest, uncaring even as her hand broke and burst apart under the combined force of her blow and collision with the dark Chaos surrounding me.

The air burst from my lungs as I bowed forward and was tossed away by the impact.

I smashed right through a lumpy, smoking rock and dug a furrow into the ground beyond before I could stop myself.

The shadows swirled with not-light for a moment as I struggled to regain my feet. Jacky would be berating me right now for my lack of martial prowess, I was sure.

My opponent's hand and forearm were already healed, and I had to literally *heave* myself to the side to avoid her next rushing attack.

She missed and stumbled, her balance thrown off. She tried to turn and follow me, but it seemed whatever she was doing to boost her speed didn't last long-term, because she grimaced in obvious frustration when I sprang away again and she couldn't keep up with me.

I struggled to relax my diaphragm enough to get air back into my lungs, then lashed out with stringy cords of night-black Chaos to keep her away from me.

This time, it broke both her legs, then constricted around them and proceeded to try and turn her lower half into hamburger.

She screamed till her voice broke.

I sympathized. Kilburn had done something similar to my arm when we fought within NIX's compound. It was more than the pain that got to you. It was the *wrongness* of your body losing its function, turning from a part of you into…meat.

To my dismay, her screams turned into hoarse laughter.

The hair on the back of my neck rose, and the dizziness grew suddenly heady, like the moment you know you've had too much to drink and are about to throw up. I took a few deep breaths of the smoky air to try and stabilize myself, and prepared for the next attack.

She raised her head to look at me, blood marring the whiteness of her smile. Despite the Chaos still stirring itself into her legs, she began to heal. It was as if my power wasn't even there. She spat out a mouthful of blood. "You are good, Godkiller, but you will never win against *me*."

I scrambled backward, but it was too late.

Her healing sped up, and with it, her entire being seemed to eschew the laws of time.

The blood disappeared, her clothing reformed, and when she rushed toward me, I knew it only by the sudden blow to my side and the rush of wind and sound that accompanied her passing. That was only the first blow.

More followed. They came from all around me, crashing into me like missiles and cratering my flesh, despite Chaos and the protection of my scales. The force was enough to knock me off my feet and into the air, but the attacks came so quickly I never had a chance to fully regain my balance or my footing.

I knew she was hurting herself. Each blow left behind some of her blood.

My vision flickered and swam after one particularly vicious blow to the back of the head, compounding the dizziness brought on by the drug.

Chaos fed the familiar ball of rage in the pit of my stomach, but instead of giving into it and lashing out, I curled into myself and turned my power toward the ground. It took almost no effort to dig a pit, fall into it, and allow the smoldering dirt to fall in on me.

Normally, burying myself alive would be a terrible strategy, but from what I'd seen of my opponent's Skill, allowing her to continue injuring herself while attacking me would just *help* her. Without me to punch, she would run out of whatever boost she got from taking damage. Hopefully, at least.

Her muffled scream reached me through the dirt. "You cannot hide forever! I can continue this till the end of time!"

I struggled to ground myself, letting Wraith inform me of my opponent's state and the layout of the battleground around us. The darkness of the back of my eyelids swirled with strange, surreal shapes. I resisted the urge to throw up as the world spun. I found some measure of control in Wraith, then dug my way back out of the ground.

Instead of relying on my physical senses, I piloted my body from the outside, as if it were a puppet. Wraith allowed me to move without stumbling, to see without confusion. The grey ash sloughed off me, mixing with the dark shroud of Chaos in the orange light of the glowing heat around us.

My opponent bared her teeth, which seemed even whiter against the darkness of her skin.

Her Skill was beautiful, in a way. Every attempt to take her down only made her more powerful.

I wondered if I should kill her. I doubted she could regrow a pulped brain or recover from decapitation. If she *could*, I probably wouldn't ever be able to win against her.

I rolled my shoulders, feeling the contusions all over my body. No, I wouldn't kill her. Unlike the battles and opponents of my past, she hadn't done anything to deserve death. She wasn't the cause of my presence in this Trial and didn't deserve to pay for my current state of desperation.

That left me with a problem. How was I supposed to defeat her without injuring her? She didn't seem to be able to empower herself or reverse time on her body without wounds to fuel her Skill, but I couldn't be absolutely sure.

Chaos swirled against my skin, and I realized the answer was all around me. Chaos was like a many-sided coin. I was not limited to destruction. What were the parameters of an "injury?" Could I just…put her to sleep? I sighed. That might work, except I had no idea how to do that safely…at least not with Chaos.

She stepped forward in challenge, her fists clenched, encouraging me to attack her.

Grinning predatorily, I walked forward very carefully, making sure to place my feet properly and keep the parts of my brain that dealt with vision and balance focused on Wraith rather than the dizzy not-light coming through my physical eyes.

When I got within range, she swung for me.

I evaded, making sure not a wisp of Chaos touched her. When she realized something was wrong and tried to fall away, I lunged toward her. My too-long fingers closed around her neck and I swung myself around behind her without letting my claws slice through the tender skin of her throat.

I restrained her with my other arm and gently pressed down on the heartbeat I could feel pulsing through her neck, forcing her head back far enough to make it difficult for her to move, but not so far to actually inflict harm to her spine.

She struggled enough to hurt herself, still, but it wasn't enough to make her stronger or faster than me, and eventually, the lack of oxygen to her brain made her eyelids flutter and the strength leave her limbs.

I knew lack of oxygen would definitely turn into physical damage within a couple minutes as death closed in on her, but if she wasn't awake to manage her Skill, would it matter? In any case, I didn't want to push it that far.

I waited a few more seconds, then looked toward the smoke-filled sky. It was so murky that I could barely see anything, but I caught a glimpse of one of the little flying cameras and heard the announcer scream out my opponent's disqualification.

The crowd's roar boiled through the arena, an echoing explosion of noise that seemed to come from every direction.

One down.

I coughed, lungs stinging from the smoke. I could barely see three meters in front of my face. Was this the other contestant's work? He was definitely versatile, but this didn't seem like his style. The smoke was so thick I doubted the cameras could even see us unless they basically rode atop our heads. That hinted at stealth, and he tended to go for a much flashier style.

I shuffled forward, extending Wraith to try and find the remaining contender. How much time had passed? I fingered the pouch on the side of my leg, muscles tensing as Wraith caught the semi-familiar forms of Red's psychedelic minions scattered around the arena. I fumbled open the pouch and grabbed the vial, but then, slowly, returned it to its resting place.

I could sense her minions.

I could also sense others sneaking about within the

obscuring smoke, but my mind slid away from that thought so slickly I wouldn't have even noticed, if not for the not-light creatures highlighting them like beacons.

"Oh," I whispered.

***

I LOOKED up as the smoke cleared for a short moment, revealing Aibhan on her raised column high above.

She met my gaze, and then the smoke filled in again. We had discussed this possibility the night before, and it looked like she still planned to let us handle things.

The thieves were converging at the far side of the arena, at the base of the butte which carried Aibhan's Well. I expected them to try and go around, or maybe climb the side of it while everyone was distracted, but instead, they seemed to be attacking the stone of the butte itself, tearing chunks of it away to create a cave in the side of the towering edifice.

"Right," I muttered to myself, the sound helping to ground me past the nausea and dizziness. "No time to waste." I used mental commands to send a Window to my teammates.

—THE CRIMSON SHADOWS ARE IN THE ARENA, HIDDEN BY THE SMOKE AND SOME SORT OF SKILL. LOOKS LIKE THEY'RE DIGGING INTO THE BASE OF AIBHAN'S BUTTE, THOUGH I'M NOT SURE WHAT THEIR PLAN IS. THE TRIAL WILL BE OVER MOMENTARILY. RED MAY NOT HAVE JUST BETRAYED US. SHE HAS A TRACKER ON EACH OF THEM, SO I'LL BE ABLE TO SEND YOU RIGHT TO THEM. WAIT FOR MY SIGNAL.—
-EVE-

—WE'RE READY.—
-ADAM-

It was pretty simple to find my final Trial rival, as he was the only one in the arena without one of Red's minions tailing him. He seemed to be as blinded by the smoke as I was, and I snuck up on him from behind.

Chaos shot forward and wrapped around him in a macabre, full-body hug. He screamed, but quickly regained control of himself and began to siphon off my power, turning it into arcs of electricity that branched off him like the dance of lightning off a Tesla coil.

I briefly contemplated the ironic coincidence that so many of my opponents in this Trial could turn my Skill against me or use it to empower themselves. But it didn't matter.

I breathed deep, then let power flow out of me along with my exhale, pulling from the Seeds that swam in my blood, that augmented my flesh and bones, and that sat in the middle of my chest underneath my sternum.

My opponent was powerful and talented, that much was obvious. To be able to control and even alter the energy of pure Chaos could not be an easy feat when my power was kin to death incarnate. Still, he was purely a mortal.

I was a godling.

Like the filament of a light bulb trying to conduct too much voltage, he reached his limit and snapped.

I withdrew Chaos immediately, and he buckled to the ground in slow-motion, electrical burns arcing across his skin and the ground around him. His heart still beat, and he was breathing.

I sighed with relief. The smoke was too thick for the announcer to immediately declare me the champion, but Aibhan would know.

—I've won.—

-Eve-

I sent the Window along with a minimap showing the layout of the arena and the location of the thieves within.

My teammates didn't hesitate.

I swayed on my feet as the side-effects of Red's drug gnawed at my consciousness, unable to see five feet in front of me, but Wraith watched as my teammates rushed in toward Aibhan's butte in a pincer formation, making sure no one could escape.

They didn't wait for me to arrive to attack. Normally, I would have been a little disappointed to miss out on the action, but with the energy I'd expended and—most importantly—the side-effects of being drugged, I was in less than stellar condition.

Nine members of the Crimson Shadows had come, which was a slightly larger number than we'd anticipated, but the lack of accurate information was just one more way the local enforcers had turned out to be less than awe-inspiring.

If everything was going according to plan, a group of enforcers, Zed, and Jacky would be attacking the criminals' hideout right now, with priority toward rescuing the captives.

All the rest of us needed to do was defeat the Crimson Shadows attacking the butte and make sure they couldn't get away.

By the time I got to the back of the arena, the battle was already well underway. As soon as I had the members of the Crimson Shadows within my physical sight, my inability to focus on them disappeared. They resolved into distinct forms, even without the not-light of Red's minions highlighting them.

The situation was slightly different than I'd expected.

—THERE'S NO ONE HERE. IT'S THE RIGHT PLACE, PRETTY SURE, BUT IT'S EMPTY.—

-JACKY-

I reached again for the vial in the pouch on my thigh, this time taking it out and downing the contents.

—THEY'RE NOT THERE BECAUSE THEY'RE ALL HERE, IT SEEMS.

I'm looking at three kids and six adults. They've got the kids working for them.—
-Eve-

—Dammit. Okay, we're gonna head your way right now.—
-Jacky-

The thieves were extremely focused on breaking through Aibhan's butte, devoting two of their nine to that while only seven defended.

An examination with Wraith revealed the reason. The base of Aibhan's Well reached all the way down through the butte, and they were attempting to puncture through to it, thereby gaining access to thousands of tons of water…along with every single artifact that had been offered to Aibhan for Trial entrance. Had that been their goal from the start? To *steal* the offerings?

Red was defending from attacks by the other Crimson Shadows while attempting to talk to the children, who didn't seem to be grateful for the ambush or receptive to her words. They were fighting back against us just as viciously as the others.

As the antidote kicked in, my dizziness and the visual distortions went away, along with my ability to perceive Red's minions. I realized only then how close I'd been to passing out. If I hadn't already built up some resistance to the effects of the hallucinogen, I probably would have been a drooling heap somewhere back in the center of the arena.

No one seemed to have noticed my arrival, occupied as they were with the mayhem of combat.

Adam and a swarm of ink constructs fought a huge, scaled creature that looked like nothing so much as a wingless dragon, with fire-breath and everything.

I assumed that was the Estreyan who'd turned into a teleporting firebird. He was some sort of multi-form shapeshifter, and the one screaming at the three children, ordering them to fight harder. *If we could take him down…*

A young earth-controller was busy digging out the base of the butte, protected by a tall man wielding a scythe. Or, perhaps, threatened into working for them by said criminal scythe-wielder?

The billowing plumes of smoke that blanketed the arena were apparently the work of one of the thieves, who was battling, and losing quite badly, to Sam.

The chain-creator, the one who'd been keeping the kids trapped in little rooms with only a bucket to relieve themselves, was fighting both Kris and Gregor, and though it was currently a stalemate, I could see a couple small marionettes sneaking up on him from behind. That fight would be over soon.

Red was busy talking to, or more aptly, pleading with, one of the children, who was surrounded by three protectors, and was herself standing protectively in front of an even smaller child. "Please, just stop fighting back. I promise, they're here to help you! Dragoon can't punish you anymore. They're here to save you from him, from them!"

It was the larger child's three guards who drew my attention, though. One of them was…Torliam? That didn't make sense. It made even less sense when I saw the other two were actually enforcers.

Then I took in Torliam's awkward movements, so unlike his normal graceful ruthlessness, and the fact he wasn't incorporating his Skill into any of his attacks against Red. The little girl was controlling all three of them. Well…*shit.*

A dispersed wave of Chaos hit the girl from the side, knocking her to the ground. Her head bounced off the hard earth and she lay still.

Her three unwilling minions regained control of themselves immediately.

The Chaos hadn't come from me, however, and as Birch,

who'd been sneakily stalking the child, pounced atop his downed prey and howled triumphantly, the tiniest child started to *wail*.

The sound was incredibly disorienting, even worse than the effects of Red's drug. It was like my mind was turning on itself, trying to convince me very, very hard that there was no one there, no one to fight, nothing to be concerned about.

Except I could see the evidence to the contrary right in front of my face, and Wraith could clearly sense that my eyes were telling the truth.

The others, it seemed, weren't quite as capable, and started wandering around like confused zombies, abandoning whatever opponent they'd been dueling.

I resisted the urge to palm my face in frustration and rushed toward the girl. Whatever she was doing, I had to stop her quickly. I tapped Torliam on the shoulder and directed him toward the mini-cave, where the final child was carving out mounds of stone and dirt. "You go handle that, I'll take care of this one."

He looked at me in confusion, but at least headed toward the cave as I'd instructed.

I clamped a hand over the small child's mouth, cutting off the sound of her wail. It didn't completely negate the effects of her Skill, but the compulsion to ignore the Crimson Shadows was diminished, merely a suggestion, not a command.

My teammates and the enforcers accompanying us regained their senses and continued with the arrests. I thought it was a pretty sure bet that this little girl's Skill had been stopping Torliam from easily tracking the Crimson Shadows, not some warding artifact as we'd originally guessed.

Next to me, Birch whined and covered his ears with his paws, sending her a baleful look.

Red rushed forward to make sure the child Birch had knocked out was alright, and yelled angrily at the enforcers who tried to handcuff the girl.

The child in my arms bit down on my palm, hard.

I didn't move my hand, since her jaw was barely strong enough to break the skin, and I'd dealt with pain much worse than this multiple times over. "You're not going to get much more out of that than a mouthful of blood," I said into her ear. "I'm not going to hurt you or the other kids, or Red." I jerked my head toward the mysterious redhead, who was ministering to the lump on the other kid's head. "She contacted me secretly so we could work together to bring the Crimson Shadows down and save you and your friends." Or at least, I was pretty sure that's what had happened. Despite the fact it all made sense now, I'd never directly discussed this with the other woman. In fact, if I'd responded differently to any of her moves, this could have gone very differently, and very, very wrong.

The child in my arms bit me again, but when that didn't work, finally calmed.

"I'm going to take my hand away. If you scream again, the hand goes right back and you're not going to get a chance to ask me any questions or talk to me. Okay?" I said.

She hesitated, then finally nodded. When her mouth was free, she spit out blood and spluttered a bit, then turned her head to glare at me. "I won't let you send me and Halsie and Baldric to the dungeons. And if you try to make the rats eat us, Halsie will just take control of them and make them eat *you*, instead!" Her voice was high-pitched and antagonistic, but the hitch at the end and the tears gathering in her eyes told the real story.

I frowned and looked around exaggeratedly. "Who said anything about dungeons? You do realize that you're a kid, right? No one is going to send you to the dungeon, and we're *definitely* not going to let any rats near you."

Torliam had set up a protective barrier between him and Scythe Guy and the child who'd been set to digging out the bottom of the Well, ensuring no backlash from the fight would be able to injure the kid. He held up a hand, and with a faint tremor of effort, clenched it into a fist as if crushing something within his fingers. A blinding flash of crushing blue energy converged on his opponent.

Scythe Guy coughed up blood and collapsed, and a few seconds later the shockwave of wind passed by me.

Adam's constructs were vicious, and he'd come prepared with *swarms* of them. Razor-sharp bird wings cut through the shape changer I'd dubbed Dragoon, and while the Estreyan tried to escape the kraken-like tentacles wrapped around him by changing forms, Adam wasn't so easily deterred.

Dragoon morphed into the smaller form of the firebird for a moment, but Adam simply smirked and moved his hand from the ink cartridges to the energy cartridge. Before Dragoon could teleport away, lightning cracked out of Adam.

I'd closed my eyes and covered the girl's with my hand so neither of us were blinded.

When I opened them again, I saw Dragoon lying on the ground, sizzling like a rotisserie chicken. Another gust of wind, this one charged with the scent of a storm, blew past, pushing away more of the smoke.

In my lap, the girl's lower lip trembled. "You're lying. Dragoon said we're bad guys now because we did bad stuff for them and if we talk about him or get caught they'll send us to the dungeons and it'll be even worse than our rooms because we won't have any buckets to go in and the rats will come when we can't hold it anymore and they'll eat us!" She took a deep breath to continue, but I pressed a clawed finger to her lips to stop her.

"He was lying," I said simply.

She blinked up at me, tears carving muddy trails down her filthy, flushed cheeks.

In the background, Torliam nudged the disabled scythe wielder with his foot, making sure the severely injured man wasn't dead. A thin crack in the base of the Well sent a spray of water geysering out of the farthest point of the newly-created cave, but the child with the earth-control power had surrendered before it got any worse.

Adam was busy holding Dragoon down while two enforcers bound him in rune-covered shackles meant to suppress his Skills.

Sam's opponent was half-catatonic, crying silently, not even struggling against his restraints.

The chain-creator had more than a few serious knife wounds courtesy of Gregor, and Kris' marionettes were holding him down while he bled out onto the ground. No one seemed particularly interested in healing him, and I noticed that Henrik "accidentally" ground the child abuser's hand into the dirt with his boot while he shackled the man's ankles together.

The girl in my arms sniffled and looked around, still wary but slightly more relaxed now. "If we're not going to the dungeon, what are you gonna do with us?"

I opened my mouth to respond with something reassuring, but my body was wracked with a sudden pain in my lower back, and my eyes rolled back in my head.

Chapter 8

I woke up to Sam's frowning face.

"We've gotta stop meeting like this," I said inanely. There had to be a limit to the number of times a person could pass out in their lives. This was becoming embarrassing.

He sighed deeply, like someone who had passed beyond irritation and was left with only fatigue. "Our illustrious apothecary Kasimir neglected to clarify kidney damage, heart palpitations, or loss of consciousness as side-effects of his 'antidote.' Also, I'm quite certain it used the base drug as a major component, which means he either had access to the source, or he's surprisingly skilled at synthesization. Which I doubt," he added, in case it wasn't clear.

I sat up and rolled my shoulders to work out some of the headache-inducing tension in my neck, then crawled reluctantly to my feet to take stock of my surroundings.

Sam moved to check on the children, who were huddled together and drinking water while hesitantly answering a female enforcer's questions.

With the smoke-creator suppressed, we were visible to the crowd and cameras again.

The announcer with the bell-covered hat, who had long since worn down all of my tolerance for his antics, was orating extra-loudly to the crowd about the same things everyone could see. Why did people need someone to explain to them what was literally happening in front of their eyes?

The hole in the side of Aibhan's butte was completely gone, fixed by her power like it had never happened.

Said goddess slithered up behind me as if on cue, her presence bringing back what tension I'd managed to release from my muscles. She got a little too close, towering above me with her half-human body.

I craned my neck back to meet her gaze.

"You have earned this, I believe," she said, somewhat reluctantly. She draped the glittering chain of the third puzzle over my shoulders. "I am sorry to part with it, but I suppose the entertainment was worth it. It would have been better had you drawn out the battle longer, and perhaps with more bloodletting, however," she added, sounding like a mother scolding their child over a mediocre report card.

"I'll...keep that in mind?"

She nodded, then turned to look at crowd seated on the other end of the arena.

Apparently, the goddess felt similarly to me about the merits of the Trial announcer, because she waved a hand and flattened his platform to cut off his constant narration. Then, her voice issuing from every rock, every ashy growth, every drop of water, she announced, "The Trial is finished."

The people quieted to a dull roar.

"A group of vulgar mortals has attempted to defile my Trial, and to steal the offerings made to my Well. I have been angered."

The dull roar petered out, and a blanket of tense silence fell over the people.

"The godling Eve-Redding spoke to me about this profanity.

She has offered me both the service of a battle for my entertainment as well as the capture and judgment of those who crossed us both. My anger is appeased. Beware, mortals. I do not forget. I will not forgive a second time."

The only sounds in the arena were the blowing of the wind and the faint pops of embers sparking and crumbling.

"Eve-Redding is the victor. According to the ancient agreement, I Bestow upon these lands the water of the Well. May it bring life and prosperity."

She turned back to us. "You may wish to move away from this place, lest you be swept away and drowned."

The locals took this very seriously, and quickly our whole group had been relocated to the higher ground on the northeastern edge of the arena.

Red, who I suddenly noticed standing just behind me, caught my eye and nodded deeply, almost smiling.

I turned so that we stood side by side to watch the proceedings together. The Crimson Shadows, except for her and the children, were bundled off with no extra fanfare, probably headed for a holding cell. Who knew what the local judiciary system was like?

When I said as much to Red, she raised her eyebrows with disbelief. "They will be executed, of course. No one will stand for the greed of a few to endanger the lives of this entire level. They will be made an example of. Some will call for torture, though that has been outlawed here for a generation now."

"Huh." They must have known that when they decided to attempt their crazed plan. Either they were extremely reckless, or they'd been extremely confident they wouldn't be caught. Which may have ended up working out for them, if not for Red. "And the children?"

"Returned to their families, if they have them and the enforcers can find them. Children like this are sometimes traded on the black market after being taken and put through a Characteristic Trial to gain a useful Skill. Most come from the poorer areas of the land, and some are even sold by their families will-ingly. If they have no family, or no family worthy of the name, another family will take them in and induct them into the bloodline."

Our attention was drawn into the distance as the water began to spill down from the top of Aibhan's butte. First a trickle, then a stream, then a roaring, crushing wall of divine force flowed down from the precipice, which left me breathless to behold.

The thundering of the water against the arena below crushed the ground and quenched the fires, throwing up a thick mist that smelled of morning dew and green things. It caught the light and the ash in the air, creating a sparkling rainbow of distinct colors.

The people were losing their minds in joy, dancing in the spray and drinking from the flow as it reached them and sped past, giving meaning to the channels carved through the land again.

I let out a shuddering breath of awe as I watched, reminded of the difference between a godling and a god.

"You planned all this?" I murmured to the woman beside me.

"I had help," she said, "but yes. I could not speak of it directly until the blood-borne power sealing my lips was removed, along with Dragoon's ability to find and punish me. I had to find some way to get your attention, and from what I have seen and read of you, the godkiller finds such a blatant challenge and offense irresistible."

I wasn't sure whether I should be chagrined or not. "You could have come to me directly and just hinted around your problem like you ended up doing."

She shook her head. "No, I could not have. But, as your earthlings say, 'all is being well that is ending well.'" She said the last in English.

Her accent was atrocious and her grammar even worse, but

I didn't correct her. "So how did you get wind of what the Crimson Shadows were doing, anyway?"

She raised an amused eyebrow. "I am a thief. A master thief. You did not think me innocent, simply because I have done a single good deed? I am part of the world of darkness, as are they."

"Master, indeed, I suppose. None of the local enforcers even seem to recognize you as a criminal. Or maybe they're just giving you a pass because you helped to bring in the others?"

She grinned, bright green eyes crinkling at the sides. "None of the others can *see* me, Eve-Redding."

I blinked a couple times, Wraith bursting into motion around us as my scales rose in alarm.

It was faint, but the shadows were a little too bright in a way that reminded me of a photo negative, and I caught a hint of disturbances in the air around us, which took the shapes of little fairies and a tentacled creature. "How?" I said aloud, letting Chaos boil just beneath my skin.

She grinned victoriously, thrilled by her reveal. "That is a secret. Perhaps I can give you a hint, even so. We are both breathing."

A tiny spray of water from the roaring deluge caught me in the eye. I blinked. When I opened my eyes again, I was alone.

Wraith caught the faint hint of something blending into my shadow and disappearing.

I pushed a couple strands of hair away from my face and let out a low chuckle. "Huh," I murmured, wondering if I should be less amused and more upset. I shrugged, settling in to watch the waters of life return to the land with the rest of my teammates.

I would tell Blue about it all when I saw him that evening. He liked interesting stories, especially if I narrated them along with fire-illustrations.

· · ·

THE STORY CONCLUDES in *Seeds of Chaos Book V: Gods of Ash and Amber.*

Go here to buy it on Amazon now: amazon.com/dp/B0813YDJYJ

Also by Azalea Ellis

Seeds of Chaos Series (Complete)

Book I: Gods of Blood and Bone

Book II: Gods of Rust and Ruin

Book III: Gods of Myth and Midnight

Gods of Smoke and Stars: A Seeds of Chaos Adventure—Available free to newsletter subscribers

Book IV: Gods of Ash and Amber

A Practical Guide to Sorcery Series

Book I: A Conjuring of Ravens

Book II: A Binding of Blood

Book III: A Sacrifice of Light

Book IV: A Foreboding of Woe — Coming Soon

Codename: Moonsable (Patreon Exclusive Sidestory)

The Honeymoon Suite (Patreon Exclusive Novelette)

The Catastrophe Collector: A Practical Guide to Sorcery Series

Book I: Larva — Coming Soon

More books may have been published since you purchased this copy.

Here's a Quick Link to All my Books.

About the Author

I'm the type of person that often has a wacky, shocking, or silly—but totally *true*—story to tell about my life.

(Like the time my brother and I were chased through a secluded strip of woods in the middle of the city, for over a mile, by a naked man with an erection.)

(Or the time a trucker threw an open bottle of pee out his passenger side window without looking right as I was walking by. You can guess what I got splashed with.)

I've got an active imagination that tends toward the outrageous and the macabre, which led to me being voted "most likely to borrow someone else's car to transport a dead body."

I write books about things that interest and excite me. I'm always in the middle of teaching myself something new, and if I'm not overwhelmingly busy I tend to get antsy. I believe that the impossible is only so if we believe it to be so. Therefore, nothing is impossible.

If you'd like to get updates from me, both about my books and about what I'm up to from time to time, the newsletter is the place to be, as I tend to be very scarce on other social media.

https://www.azaleaellis.com/newsletter/

For more information:
www.azaleaellis.com
author@azaleaellis.com